A CANDLELIGHT ECSTASY ROMANCE

"Don't be afraid of me, or of yourself," he whispered. "Don't be afraid to be a woman and to love me completely."

Kristen was shaken by the violence of her emotions. She wanted with a sudden desperation to tell him what he wanted to hear: that she loved him, and yes! that she desired him. But she forced back the words. To say them would destroy all her defenses against him and leave herself open.

But now his whispers were causing her to lose control; his kisses and caresses were becoming more intimate. She fought down a growing panic. No man had ever demanded this of her with such overwhelming determination; no man had ever torn aside her barriers, stripped her emotions bare as Clay was doing now. . . .

CANDLELIGHT ECSTASY ROMANCES

Dear Reader:

In response to your enthusiasm for Candlelight Ecstasy Romances, we are now increasing the number of titles per month from two to three.

We are pleased to offer you sensuous novels set in America depicting modern American women and men as they confront the provocative problems of a modern relationship.

Throughout the history of the Candlelight line, Dell has tried to maintain a high standard of excellence, to give you the finest in reading pleasure. It is now and will remain our most ardent ambition.

Vivian Stephens
Editor
Candlelight Romances

BESIEGED BY LOVE

Maryann Young

A CANDLELIGHT ECSTASY ROMANCE

Published by
Dell Publishing Co., Inc.
1 Dag Hammarskjold Plaza
New York, New York 10017

Copyright © 1981 by Maryann Young

Dell ® TM 681510, Dell Publishing Co., Inc.

ISBN: 0-440-10581-1

Printed in the United States of America
First printing—July 1981

CHAPTER 1

Kristen stepped out of the small camp trailer and stood for a moment looking about her. It was midmorning now and the chill of the night had been dispelled as the sun made its way slowly up and over the mountaintops and strove to press its rays into the valley below.

The third week in August, she thought incredulously, and summer was in its last days here in the Mogollons. She was surprised that the time had passed so quickly, but then, these summer holidays never seemed to last nearly long enough.

Leaning back against the rough trunk of the tree, she let the quiet wrap around her, soothe her as it always could. So different from the rush, rush days of finals and the tight schedules of the last days of classes. Very much she enjoyed these yearly outings with Beth, her sister, and Brian, her sister's professor husband. Ever since Beth had married four years earlier, Kristen had been accompanying them on these out-in-the-woods adventures and they had become high points in her all too normal life.

Stepping back into the compact camp trailer, she went into the small bathroom and dug around until she found the shampoo. Beth and Brian had left camp with the dawn to make an exploration into the mountains on their trail bike and were not expected to return until lunch. Rather Kristen did not expect them back until time for supper, for Brian was an inveterate stopper and looker, and therefore a thirty-minute trip could easily be stretched into several hours. So Kristen never expected them back until darkness drove them. The more practical Beth could usually be counted on to see that they were not caught out after the last rays of the sun.

Walking to the creek, she sank down on a large flat rock at the bank and watched the clear water as it ran swiftly into the various pools that had been created by logs fallen across the stream. Then, kicking off her sneaker, she placed an experimental toe into the water and then jerked it quickly out.

Shivering now, she hesitated, running her fingers through her hair, debating with herself as to whether she really wanted to do this. Then resolutely she sighed and shook her head. Her hair was in desperate need of a good wash, and the cold water notwithstanding, she was going to wash it.

Taking a deep breath, unscrewing the cap from the shampoo bottle, and securing her towel within easy reach, she stretched out across the flat rock and quickly, before she could think better of it, dipped her head into the icy waters. Involuntarily she gasped and pulled her head up quickly. It had been much worse than she had expected. Cold water ran down her face and trickled down her back, soaking her knit blouse, plastering it to her skin and chilling her to the bone.

Without a second thought she pulled the wet blouse off over her head and draped it upon an overhanging limb above her head where it could dry while she resumed her hair washing. She had become so accustomed to the fact that they went for days on end in these out of the way parts without seeing a soul that she thought nothing of sitting on the side of the creek without her blouse.

"Well, hello."

Kristen's head and face were now covered by the towel, and when the voice sounded, she straightened up quickly, dropping the towel, and turned to see who had spoken. There, standing only a few feet away and staring back at her, stood a man. It was the obviously interested gleam in his eye that caused her to remember, and with acute embarrassment, her lack of attire, and that sent her scrambling hastily to retrieve her soggy blouse.

While she struggled to disentangle the garment from the tree limb where it had become hopelessly entangled, she told herself frantically that she had just as much on as she would if she were wearing a bathing suit and was indeed covered much more than if she had been dressed in some she had seen, and she tried to maintain a calm exterior and to ignore the eyes that she knew never left her for a moment.

She\gave the blouse a final jerk, snagging the knit, and pulled it over her head.

The newcomer was certainly very intent on his observations; he was watching with an open smile of appreciation. Her long legs encased in the white shorts accentuating their tan, the wet blouse clinging like her skin, the dark brown hair almost black now that it was wet, curling damply around her face, now flushed a bright pink from embarrassment and anger.

"And just what are you doing here?" she demanded to know in a choked voice.

His eyebrows raised slightly. "Fishing," he put forth calmly. "And I've always considered the scenery hereabouts to be breathtaking, but I must say it has improved this year. I don't believe I've ever seen—"

Kristen tried to leap to her feet, but she missed her footing on the slippery rock, thereby losing some of her dignity, plus one of her sneakers. It fell into the water. She bent over to get it, but he was faster and in a few rapid strides he had grasped the shoe where it had floated downstream and in a matter of seconds was holding the dripping footwear out to her.

9

With as much good grace as she could muster she put out her hand, muttering her thank you in tones as icy as the water that now dripped from the shoe as she took it from him. She looked up into his face and found that although he was not smiling his eyes were twinkling maddeningly.

Despite the embarrassment she felt at having been caught half-dressed, she found herself studying the face above hers. The skin was deeply tanned with sun-wrinkles at the corners of his eyes; the brown hair was sunstreaked. Obviously the man spent much time out of doors. The eyes, staring directly into hers with such disconcerting directness, were of a color somewhere between brown and gold.

She frowned. This chance meeting was rapidly getting out of hand. Even the coldness of her voice and the obvious displeasure of her expression did nothing whatever to quell this fellow. She turned and started to make her way back toward the trailer, hoping he would take the hint and get lost, but surprisingly enough he fell into step beside her.

"Do you come here often?" he asked with a calm matter-of-factness that for the moment left her speechless. He was impossible! A man who walks up on a woman half-dressed and, instead of leaving without having made his presence known, not only stands around watching while she dresses but remains for pleasant conversation—it was too much.

She whirled around and was on the verge of telling him a few things when she heard the faint sound of the trail bike and then Beth and Brian appeared around the bend of the trail. Brian maneuvered the bike within a few feet of them, and as he changed the gears, Beth jumped off, waving gaily.

"We're back! I forgot to pack a lunch," she explained,

allowing her brilliant smile to bless first Kristen and then the man who was standing beside her.

Pulling the bike back up on its stand, Brian looked about with his usual bland stare. "I don't know why she intended to pack a lunch in the first place," he said, honestly puzzled. "I told her we'd be back here for lunch."

Beth grinned and shook her head despairingly. "If I'd packed a lunch, we'd still be heading over the next rise. Only the fact of missing the all-important meal brought us back." She stepped to the man standing beside Kristen and held out her hand. "I'm Beth Hartley, Kristen's sister, and this is my husband, Brian. You been fishing?" she asked, glancing at the rod lying on the ground.

The man smiled and nodded, shaking hands first with Beth and then with Brian.

"That's right. I'm Clay Courtney and I just happened along in time to see . . ." He paused and glanced toward Kristen's widening eyes. ". . . just in time to see your sister's shoe fall into the creek and to come to her rescue, or rather to the shoe's."

Kristen smothered an impulse to comment. "And I'm Kristen Ames," she introduced herself and nodded with as much courtesy as she could muster and once again started toward the trailer. She could have strangled her friendly sister when she heard her offering to fix coffee and would he like to have some?

And of course he accepted with obvious pleasure.

The four of them made their way into the trailer and Beth began busying herself at the small butane stove.

"What part of Texas are you from?" Beth asked as they sat together in the small booth, having been quick to catch a kindred accent.

"I'm from the hill country," Clay answered around a mouthful of cheese, "down near San Antonio." His eyebrows, the most communicative and mobile part of his countenance, lifted as Beth squealed delightedly.

11

"How wonderful. Kristen's going to be in San Antonio for the next nine months or so. So isn't it nice that in all this vast country you two should meet."

Kristen cast a darkling look toward her sister.

Ignoring the look, Beth continued: "What do you do in the hill country, Clay?"

"I've got a ranch, nothing really outstanding, mind you, in Bexar County south of San Antonio. And it's growing right along—got some good stock. I have a partner and between us we keep things going."

Beth glanced toward Kristen, who was remaining strangely silent; she had turned her entire attention, seemingly, toward her eating, which was unusual. Beth had never known her to stay so completely out of a conversation before.

"We're from a small town in the center of the state—Marshalton," Beth went on doggedly. "Kristen has been studying at the college there for the past three years, but she's taking the next year off to work with an historian in San Antonio. She's really the brain of our family, except for Brian, of course." She turned to gaze with fondness toward her husband, who seemed to be completely oblivious of the conversation going on around him and was munching in an abstract manner on whatever Beth set in front of him.

"I met Brian at the university at Austin, where he was the professor of one of my courses. He saw almost at once that I wasn't nearly smart enough to ever get my degree, so he took pity and married me."

Brian came out of his fog briefly. "She is smart enough but definitely not of a scholarly nature," he corroborated in his detached manner, "but she does have her compensations," he added with a bemused grin.

Beth dimpled prettily. "Well, thank you, darling. That was very nicely said. Anyway, Kristen is going to work for

12

this historian, as I said, for a year, doing just what I don't know."

Beth looked at her sister with something akin to disgust. Why was her usually smart sister allowing this beautiful opportunity to slip through her fingers? Clay's eyebrows lifted and a certain spark of humor lighted the brown-gold eyes; the crinkles at the corners deepened.

Feeling they had discussed her as if she were absent long enough, and spurred on by the fact that they were discussing her favorite subject, Kristen spoke at last, much to her sister's relief.

"Mrs. Faraday's a writer, primarily," she began, "but she's also interested in the restoration of the missions of Texas. She writes articles, does mountains of research, writes historical novels, collects different artifacts and statuary, which are then restored to their original positions in the various missions. I was offered the position as her assistant for the next few months and I thought it would be advantageous for me to take her up on her offer. I'm anxious to live in San Antonio. We visited there once with our aunt and uncle when we were younger and I can still remember being fascinated with the city—its history is so varied."

Unable to resist a sideways glance, Kristen found that Clay was studying her intently, and she quickly jerked her head back around.

When the somewhat uninspired meal was finished, Brian got to his feet and began to putter about the trailer in what other people might think to be a distracted manner, but Beth and Kristen had long since discovered that organization took a different form with Brian. He soon completed his meanderings to announce that he had all the tools and odd paraphernalia that he thought to be necessary for the completion of the interrupted outing of the morning and suggested that he and Beth be on their way.

"There are some marvelous rock formations, also some

13

plants I'd like to study further," he muttered to Clay as his form of apology for his abrupt departure.

Beth looked hesitatingly from Clay to Kristen and then back to Clay again. He appeared to be trustworthy enough, but then one never knew these days. But it wasn't as if Kristen were still a child, for heaven's sake. But all the same . . .

Clay's eyebrows moved and his eyes glinted. "I'm going to be fishing on down the stream for a while and I'd like Kristen to come with me, if she doesn't have anything else to do." He grinned suddenly. "I'm harmless enough—usually—and I'd like to have her company."

Unused to such handling of her affairs, Kristen felt herself bristling. "Thank you, I'm sure," she said with some spirit, "but I don't like to fish. I—"

Clay cut smoothly across her words. "I don't expect you to fish if you don't want to. I just said that I'd like to have your company while I did. That is, unless you've got some further plans for soaping up the stream. In that case I'll forgo the fishing and just hang around and watch."

Beth turned to Kristen with a puzzled look, appeared to be about to question her, but Kristen spoke hurriedly. "On further thought," she said resignedly. "I guess I wouldn't mind just walking along with you. It's a lovely day and a walk would be nice. And I really have nothing better to do," she finished lamely.

Beth frowned. Kristen's words sounded right enough, but her expression and her tone were something else again. Once again Beth started to speak, but at that moment Brian gave the motorbike a kick of the crank and the purr of the motor reminded her that her husband was waiting. She cast a quick look back over her shoulder toward Clay, whose very innocence seemed guilty, and then she shrugged. If Kristen was not able to take care of herself by now, she never would be, so she ran over to hop astraddle of the bike and waved as they went off down the trail.

They were just barely out of earshot when Kristen turned on Clay wrathfully.

"How dare you do that to me!" she demanded in quivering tones.

"How dare I do what to you?" inquired Clay blandly.

"How dare you blackmail me!"

"How so?"

"Don't you play innocent with me." Her voice was tight and her fists were clenched at her sides. "Soap the stream, indeed!"

Kristen turned to walk away, but Clay reached out and grasped her arm, holding her back.

"You're going with me for company, remember?"

Kristen, who had said all that to Beth just to get rid of her, looked around wide-eyed. Did he really think she was going to go with him? She was aghast at his nerve.

Half an hour later, walking along the embankment of the stream, watching as Clay expertly cast his line into the swift waters, she was still wondering how she came to be there. She had fully intended to brush him off with a cold disdain, which had always been highly successful in the past with other men. And she *had* tried. But Clay Courtney simply was not as other men and it just had not worked; he had refused to be brushed aside and here she was now keeping him company while he fished.

Not that he gave her a moment's notice, she thought, nettled. She might as well be back soaping the stream for all the attention he was paying her. But with his attention so thoroughly absorbed in his fishing she took the opportunity to give further study to this strange man who had entered her life so abruptly.

He was not as young as most of the men she knew; she surmised he was probably in his late twenties. Although he was tall, the broadness of his frame made him appear shorter. He was solidly built; the brown forearms rippled as he drew back the rod and then threw it forward again.

15

He seemed very much at home out of doors and she could not imagine him working anywhere else. He fit very neatly into her conception of what a rancher should look like.

Perching herself on a fallen log and half-closing her eyes, she tried to picture him riding a horse. Though more probably, she thought ruefully, he rode his range in a Jeep or a pickup. Progress marching ever onward.

"You're frowning again," he accused her. "You'll end up with a face full of wrinkles if you're not careful."

Her eyes flew open. He had abandoned the stream and was standing directly in front of her, looking down at her with an eyebrow cocked.

"You know, I bet you'd be really attractive if you'd try smiling once in a while."

Kristen got to her feet. "Thank you, I think," she snapped. "And as far as that goes, I might have been smiling my silly head off for the last hour and you wouldn't have been in the least aware of it."

Instantly she regretted having said the words, for his eyes began to sparkle. She had sounded as if she had wanted him to look at her, to notice her, this rude, over-bearing, arrogant, assuming—

"I knew well enough what you were doing," he assured her, "but I was thinking."

"Oh?" she said, but he did not elaborate further and this served to increase her irritation. She turned away from him, but he pulled her back.

"You know, you can be a very disturbing element on a fishing trip. I usually have my limit by this time."

Standing very close to him, she could see the brown flecks in the gold eyes, the white teeth against the dark skin, the sunstreaked hair. In spite of herself her breath quickened.

With one movement his face was closer to hers.

"This is against my usually good judgment," he murmured with a certain fierceness that was incongruous with

16

the softness of the kiss that followed. Then he released her suddenly and bent to pick up the fishing rod that had dropped to the ground and fastened his entire attention to the untangling of the line.

The kiss, coming on the heels of being seemingly ignored, had been a surprise and Kristen used the time to gather her distracted wits. She felt strangely young and confused, as if this kiss were her first, which was ridiculous. She had been kissed many times, and often quite expertly, but somehow this one had been different and it left her somewhat shaken.

When the line had been restored to working order, Clay turned and regarded her for a long moment; his scrutiny was such that it caused Kristen to frown, vaguely puzzled. She was not sure exactly what she had expected from him, but this calm, somewhat stern appraisal was disconcerting.

Presently he grasped his rod firmly, turned, and started retracing his steps back up along the edge of the creek. His step was unhurried but firm and purposeful; he did not resume his fishing. After he had taken a few steps, he turned and glanced back over his shoulder where she remained unmoving, staring after him.

"Aren't you coming?" he asked evenly.

His terse question stirred her to action and she fell into step beside him on the narrow trail. They walked along in a peculiar and uneasy silence, or so it seemed to Kristen. But not so with Clay, who seemed relaxed and absorbed in his own thoughts while Kristen's were varied, mumbled, and distracted. Never before had she been kissed so thoroughly and then forgotten with equal thoroughness, and it was a new experience for her. She was too surprised by it all to be embarrassed.

The silence of the walk back to camp was unbroken except for the sounds of the forest around them and the steady crunching of their footsteps along the pathway.

Once she had stumbled over a stone in the path, had lost her footing, and Clay had had to steady her, but once she had regained her balance, he had released her quickly and had walked on at a slightly quickened pace.

Beth and Brian had not returned when they reached the trailer, and while Kristen was debating with the idea of whether or not she should ask him in for coffee, he solved her problem for her and with dispatch.

"Tell your sister and her husband thanks for the lunch. And even though you're far too distracting to be a good fishing partner, thanks for going along with me—even when you didn't want to. And the best of luck in San Antonio."

He had been standing just a step away from her and Kristen thought for a moment he was going to reach for her, but after a fraction of hesitation he turned and was gone.

CHAPTER 2

Kristen sat in the back seat of the car in a profound silence. They had remained at Willow Creek for two days after Clay's abrupt departure and he had not returned. Now, as they made their way homeward, Kristen spent the time reliving the afternoon she had spent with Clay Courtney and struggling to make some sense of it.

Now that she had had time to think about it, she had not been too surprised when he had kissed her. She had been around enough to know that he would more than likely make some sort of pass, considering the circumstances. But to kiss her as soundly as he had and then to leave so abruptly was at best puzzling. Looking back, she could not figure whether she had been intrigued by him before he had behaved so strangely or afterward *because* of his strange behavior. But intrigued, she admitted finally, she definitely was.

And just exactly what had he meant by that cryptic remark he had made just before he kissed her? What did he mean "against my usually good judgment"?

With relief she saw the outskirts of Marshalton beginning to pass her window. Quiet, calm, uncomplicated Marshalton with her quiet, uncomplicated Aunt Maude and Uncle Frank. She had grown up here in this town, she and Beth. She had been only two years old and Beth five when their parents had been killed in the crash of their private plane. Their mother's sister, Maude, had taken them without so much as a hesitation and had brought them up with their own child, a son, Martin, who had been ten years old at the time of the accident.

Martin had married and was now working with an oil company in South America; Beth had done the unexpected and had gone away to Austin to the university, where she promptly met and married Brian. So it had been tacitly agreed that Kristen should remain at home and attend the smaller local college. She had been agreeable to this arrangement, liking Marshalton well enough, and several of her friends from high school had remained. She loved her aunt and uncle as much as she could have loved real parents—probably more, for they had never treated either Beth or herself as anything but their own. They had brought them up as if they had been born into the family; never had they felt for a moment as if they were intruders or outsiders, nor had Maude or Frank ever acted as if they regretted their adoption of the two orphaned girls.

Their life had been simple and ordinary. Uncle Frank had owned a grocery store; Aunt Maude had taken care of the large, white house and the three children, nursing them through all the various childhood diseases and heartaches, and done it with a serenity that had been unruffled but not unfeeling. Therefore, it was always good to return home to Marshalton.

It was midafternoon when Brian maneuvered the car and trailer up to the curb in front of the Ames house. Seconds later Aunt Maude stepped out onto the porch and waited patiently until her children had emerged and then swept them into her embrace.

"You've just missed your Uncle Frank," she told them as she ushered them into the living room. "He went back down to the store. He keeps telling himself that Roger knows what he's doing and then goes down just to make absolutely sure that he does. Retirement comes hard to a man who's been busy all his life."

She spoke indulgently and Kristen was glad to hear her speak Roger's name without hesitation. Not only was Roger buying her uncle's store, a supermarket now of some size, but he and Kristen had dated somewhat steadily during the last year and their relationship was fast becoming a family affair. Certainly her aunt and uncle would be happy should she find herself in love with Roger; it would mean one of their children would be sure to locate in Marshalton, but realizing this was a purely selfish reason, they had said nothing. It would be her own decision to make; they would never seek to persuade. Still she sometimes sensed the pressure, even if it was self-imposed.

The next day Beth and Brian left for Austin in order to get settled in before fall enrollment; Kristen set herself to the task of getting her clothes in order for her move to San Antonio.

Also she needed time to think before she came face to face with Roger. She did not know how she felt about him, but then, she had never been given to strong feelings where men were concerned. She had known Roger for many years, dating him during high school days and then on into college, and she supposed her feelings for him had been stronger than they had been for anyone else. He was easy to get along with, treated her with a deference she had come to expect.

But she did not want to make any decisions about him, not yet. She had her work in San Antonio to think of and her schooling to finish. Marriage would have to wait its turn; there was not any rush. But she could not ask Roger to wait until she was ready. It was not fair to him.

During this time she refused to allow herself to think of Clay Courtney. He had been only a brief, and somewhat disturbing, interlude that was well over and done with. He had not fit into the pattern she had laid out for her life and she brushed him aside with a firm resolution.

* * *

21

A light knock sounded on her bedroom door and she turned her attention from the dresses piled on the bed.

"Yes?"

The door opened and Aunt Maude stepped into the room, glanced quickly about, and shook her head. Every possible place in the room, bed, chairs, chests, window-seat, was piled with skirts, blouses, sweaters, dresses, and underwear. Drawers were pulled open and stood completely bare. The dressing table was cluttered with bottles, jars, containers of every size and shape. Having run out of space, Kristen dumped the slacks she had piled in her arms into a heap in a corner.

Aunt Maude sighed as she looked around. "It appears you're going away and you don't ever plan to return."

The statement was said lightly, but Kristen was quick to note the undertone of sadness in the words. She went to her foster mother and hugged her close.

"Of course not," she chided her. "It's just that I thought I'd take everything out and give it a good looking over so I'd know exactly what I wanted to take and what I wanted to leave here." She observed the various piles with despair. "But now I can't seem to make heads or tails out of it all."

Aunt Maude shook her head. "You're working at it too hard." Then she added, "Roger's downstairs and wants to know if you've got a minute."

"Sure. Tell him I'll be right down."

After Maude had gone, Kristen turned to the littered dressing table and ran a hasty comb through her hair. With this done she did not feel quite so messy and was able to walk down the stairs with a smile and enter the room with outstretched hands. He was standing in the living room with his hands clasped firmly behind him, gazing into the empty fireplace, and jerked around as she entered, taking her hands into both of his. He held them for a long moment while his eyes searched her face.

22

"I can't have changed much, Roger." She smiled at him. "I've only been gone a few weeks."

His dark eyes lingered on hers; he still held her hands firmly. "Just a few weeks," he repeated slowly. "It seems longer."

She caught the note in his voice and something inside her responded to it. "Well, I have managed to get myself a nice tan, if you'll notice. But enough about me. Tell me about the store. Uncle Frank says you're doing great."

Roger had worked for Frank Ames ever since he had been in high school, working after school and Saturdays; after he had shown his abilities, it had been understood that one day he would take over the business from Frank.

"The store's doing great," he answered, but he was not to be put off his course. "I'd like to take you out some evening, Kristen, before you leave."

"Of course, Roger. I'd like that very much."

When the day she was to leave finally came, Kristen welcomed it. Her evening with Roger had been nice; he had neither pressured her nor had he asked anything she could not give. But she could not come to a firm conclusion and therefore she thought it best to get away. Although she strove to hide her eagerness from her aunt and uncle, she was sure her foster mother's practiced eye spotted it. She drove away amid admonitions to drive carefully and to write often.

She shed Marshalton as if thrusting aside a burden and tried to focus her entire attention upon the highway before her and San Antonio at its end.

CHAPTER 3

Kristen stopped for lunch at a small restaurant on the outskirts of San Antonio. She would need all the fortification possible before tackling the freeway leading into the sprawling city, for here was another piece of progress she was unsure of and it filled her with a cold apprehension.

So she had taken the letter from her purse while she lingered over her coffee and checked the address for the dozenth time, firmly planting it in her memory. She also studied the city map once again.

Mrs. Faraday lived in one of the older sections of the town in an old house she had rented for her stay in San Antonio, for the historian was not a native of either San Antonio or of Texas. She had come to Texas from a stay in New Mexico and Arizona, where she had been doing a series of articles and a book or two based on the history of the Indians in the two states. The house she had rented was hopefully large, for Kristen was to live there, along with another assistant Mrs. Faraday had hired last May. Kristen was curious about this other assistant; all she knew was that he or she was also a student. She was also anxious to meet Mrs. Faraday, a widow who had all the earmarks of being a very interesting person.

A short while later, bringing her small car to a stop in front of the number she had been seeking, she sat for a few moments just staring. The house was not simply large, it was huge. And it was old, probably of antebellum vintage;

the fresh coat of white paint doing little to mask its age. The front porch was at least four or five feet from the ground with a half-dozen steps leading up to it; there were two stories, with a window or two above the second that might have been a third story or only attics. A porch was across the front on both the first and second stories and they had been almost mercilessly covered with the various gingerbread trimmings popular at the time of the house's construction.

And Kristen loved it immediately. Reaching to open the car door, she stepped out as if in a trance without taking her eyes from the breathtaking edifice before her. She checked the house number once again for fear she had been mistaken and was relieved to find the number coincided with the one in the letter.

Mounting the steps, she glanced around the porch and then pressed her finger to the button; she would have preferred an immense door knocker, but one must not halt the march of progress.

After only a short moment soft footsteps could be heard and then the door was opened by a short, Mexican woman, who smiled, white teeth flashing. "Yes?"

Returning the smile, Kristen spoke. "I'm Kristen Ames. Mrs. Faraday is expecting me."

The woman's smile widened and she stepped aside, motioning for Kristen to enter. "*Sí*, the señora expects the Señorita Ames."

Kristen stepped past the woman into a long hallway that she could see reached the entire length of the house into the kitchen. The hallway itself was wide and roomy but was thoroughly cluttered with furnishings of many and varied types. There was also a wide stairway beginning at the left of the hallway and curving up over the hallway below and disappearing into another hallway above. The wood of the paneling and the floors, where it

25

was not covered with woven rugs of intricate and colorful designs, shone even in the darkened room.

The Mexican woman had stepped to a large door on the right of the entry hall and was tapping lightly; Kristen heard the faint answer and the door was thrown open. The room into which Kristen was ushered was even more cluttered, if that was possible, than was the hallway, and although the room was large, the fact that it contained two couches, which flanked a fireplace against the opposite wall, a daybed of sorts along the front window, several chairs of different styles and sizes, and tables loaded with statuary and bric-a-brac, seemed to diminish its size.

Seated on one of the couches, almost obliterated by the furnishings, was a small woman with neatly styled gray hair and very black and sparkling eyes. She rose as Kristen entered, and despite her frail, birdlike appearance, the clasp into which she took Kristen's hand was firm.

"You're Kristen Ames, I take it," she said with a smile that set her dark eyes dancing. "That's fine, fine. I have awaited your coming with much eagerness. There's much work here to be done and I'm fairly itching to get started."

Kristen, spurred on by the woman's enthusiasm and her own, replied, "I'm delighted to be here, Mrs. Faraday, and I'm sure I'm every bit as anxious to begin as you are. I just hope I'll prove to be of some help to you in your work. It sounds very interesting."

Mrs. Faraday gestured for her to be seated and Kristen skirted a table laden with several of what she recognized to be the kachina dolls of the Hopi Indians; there were also several clay pots decorated with the Navajo symbol of the thunderbird. She sat down on the couch opposite her new employer, eying her over a coffee table crowded about with other relics.

"Have you had lunch?" Mrs. Faraday inquired, and when Kristen had assured her she had eaten, the older woman turned to the Mexican woman, who was still standing in the doorway. "If you would please bring coffee, Maria Rosa, I think that should be all we'll need. And send Alicia in when she returns."

Maria Rosa nodded and left. Mrs. Faraday resumed her place on the couch and looked across to Kristen. "I'll need to tell you right now that Maria Rosa doesn't speak very much English. She does understand a fair amount of what you say to her if you're careful not to speak too rapidly and not to use too many of the more complicated words, but she has trouble speaking it. Otherwise she's a rare jewel and cooks some marvelous dishes. She and her husband, Ramon, have been so helpful. I don't know what I would have done without them.

"But the poor man—Ramon, I mean. He follows orders well enough, but I'm not sure his thought processes are all they might be. But I think that comes from his allowing his wife to do all his thinking for him. She does keep him fairly well under her thumb, but he's marvelous to help around the house and the gardens outside."

She stopped and fluttered her hands as if to erase all that she had said.

"He's a good man for all of that. And now to business. I'll give you the rest of the day to unpack and to get accustomed to the house, and then bright and early, and I do mean early, for I've found my mind, which I fear is aging just as the rest of me, is much sharper during the early hours, we shall get to work."

Kristen looked at her new employer with interest; somehow she was not quite as she had expected her to be. But she was not disappointed. Mrs. Faraday could have been any age from fifty to eighty, but her eyes were alert and she showed none of the slowness or vagueness that comes to some in later years. The dark eyes were sharp and quick and the small hands gestured with the firmness that had been present in the handclasp.

"You'll take down my notes and type them for me," she

went on briskly, "and you'll aid me with my research, which means, I fear, delving through thick and sometimes monotonous volumes for some small detail. I tend to be a horrid stickler for detail, I'm afraid."

Kristen interpolated that she would not mind the research; it was something she herself enjoyed very much.

"That is fine, my dear, fine. Then I think we shall get along famously, I'm sure. Some of your research can be done here, for I have a fairly well-stocked library of my own"—she waved her hand vaguely about—"but you will, of course, spend many hours in the library in the city."

Kristen nodded and Mrs. Faraday went on. "I have another girl in my employ at present, as I told you in our correspondence. Her name is Alicia and she's from Saltillo, Mexico. She's been attending the university in Mexico City, but like yourself she's pausing in her studies for a while. But not, I think, for the same reason as yourself. Her parents cannot continue to pay her way, so she's working to save some money to continue her studies on her own."

Kristen murmured that this was to her credit and Mrs. Faraday nodded. "She doesn't have the same duties as yourself. As you've no doubt noticed—unless you're half blind," she added with a smile, "I've collected many and various items in the way of furniture and other things. I become quite involved with my subjects that I'm writing about and I collect objects that go along with the subject matter. It is Alicia's duty to help me with my collections, to catalog the different items of her country that come into my possession." Her hands fluttered toward the gaily woven rugs at their feet and the pottery scattered about; there were also several beautifully painted pictures lining the walls.

"I've just finished an extended stay among the Indians of New Mexico and Arizona. And I found their work absolutely fascinates me, but then I fully expect to be

28

equally fascinated with the Mexican culture of San Antonio."

If her Mexican fascination came anywhere near to equaling the Indian one, Kristen thought, looking about her, she's going to have to find even a larger house than this one.

Mrs. Faraday got to her feet. "I'll have Ramon bring in your suitcases and take them up to your room. Then we'll have a quick run through the house—it's rather large and rambling and an initial guided tour might help you to become better oriented."

Kristen waited eagerly for the woman's return, for she was positively aching to go through the old house. Even despite the clutter, or perhaps because of it, the house had a certain charm that reached out to Kristen's imagination.

Following in Mrs. Faraday's wake, Kristen passed from the large living room through tall double doors that reached entirely to the high ceiling, into an equally large dining room. The dining table and chairs could have been the same ones that had belonged to the original owners of the house. There was a large fireplace to the right of the room with more double doors on the left, which Kristen surmised opened into the large hallway.

She let her hand move along the polished wood of the bannister as they climbed the wide stairway and noticed how well worn the wood had become from the many hands that had done just as hers were doing now. She wondered as she always did in similar circumstances about the people who had walked along here before her.

The second floor consisted of a long hallway with the doors leading to the bedrooms and there was another small stairway leading to the bedroom in which Maria Rosa and Ramon slept, and also the attic.

"Filled with various and sundry items I've collected during my ramblings of the past years. When you no longer have a husband and there are no children to occupy

29

the empty spaces, then you tend to fill them with the trivial."

Kristen felt a sudden compassion, for the words were spoken with a certain poignancy, but before she could speak, Mrs. Faraday continued in the brisk tone Kristen was to learn to associate with her.

"You may retire now to your room and begin getting your things in order. I'm sure Ramon has brought them in from the car, but if not, all you need to do is call out. Take your time, and as I said, call out if there's anything you need."

With a nod she made her way back down the stairs and Kristen turned the knob of the door Mrs. Faraday had indicated was to be hers. It was with some relief that Kristen saw that all the clutter of downstairs had not made its way into her quarters. Her room was large, as were all the rooms, but here there were great patches of open space the others did not contain. And her room was also free of the souvenirs of her employer's past. Thankfully she saw that there were no statues or pottery.

Her suitcases were lying on the chest at the end of the bed and on the floor beside it but Kristen ignored them for the moment and crossed to the window and drew back the heavy drapes. She gazed out across the tops of the trees and the roofs on the buildings of San Antonio with a deep sense of satisfaction. She was here and the old city, nearly two hundred and fifty years of history in its wake, lay waiting for her.

Her glance dropped and she saw to her surprise and delight that the river ran just below her window; the house was obviously built almost right upon it. Leaning forward, she pressed her face against the windowpane and watched the water as it moved slowly and easily, as it had been doing for centuries, its banks a profusion of palmettos and aladiums.

Tugging the window open, she felt a warm breeze laden

with the scent of flowers brush against her cheek. Looking down, she could see the corner of a small garden. Someone, Ramon most likely, had taken time to plant flowers and the warm, humid climate had done the rest, and to perfection.

She had perched herself upon the windowsill, drinking in the faint, mingling perfumes, when a knock sounded on her door. Expecting to see Maria Rosa, she called out but looked around to find a younger Mexican girl standing in the doorway. Surprised, she could only stare for a long moment. Even though she was dressed in a simple pair of slacks and a shirt, with her long black hair, brown eyes, and olive complexion she still looked exactly like an enlarged replica of all the Spanish dolls Kristen had ever seen.

When the Mexican girl spoke, her pronunciation was that of someone who has learned the language through schooling and not from everyday use.

"You are Kristen Ames."

It was not stated as a question, but Kristen nodded. She was a little taken aback, for she thought she could detect a faint note of antagonism in the tone of the girl's voice.

"And you must be Alicia," she said smiling. "Mrs. Faraday told me that—"

"*Si,* I am Alicia Rodriguez. Mrs. Faraday said I should come up and we should become acquainted."

Yes, there it was again and the antagonism was even more pronounced. She was making it quite plain that she was there only because Mrs. Faraday had told her to come and for no other reason. But why should this girl resent her? Was she afraid she had come to take her job away from her?

"I hear we'll be working together," Kristen began, hoping to reassure the girl.

But Alicia's eyes hardened as she looked at Kristen. "My work will be quite different from yours," she said

31

before Kristen could speak further. "I know nothing about reading through dusty old books." The contempt was obvious. "I will help the señora with her collections. I understand the art of my country."

And that puts you in your place quite neatly, Kristen told herself with a small smile. "Well, that's just fine," she said easily, trying not to let this conversation bother her. This girl seemed bound to stir up some sort of hard feelings. "Then we shouldn't need to bother one another, for I can assure you that I don't know a dime's worth about art of any kind—Mexican or otherwise."

With that she slid off the windowsill and moved toward her suitcases.

"I'm sure you'll excuse me while I unpack and you can go assure Mrs. Faraday that we've become acquainted."

Kristen grabbed up a suitcase and swung it upon the bed and began pulling things out, acting as if Alicia were no longer present, but still watching her covertly from the corner of her eye.

The Mexican girl hesitated in the doorway, glancing back toward Kristen as if undecided what to do next. Then she took a tentative step back into the room.

"I can be of some help?"

The question was, Kristen supposed, as close to a grudging apology as the girl could muster. This sudden change of tactics left Kristen a little bewildered. The girl obviously resented her being there and this was regretful since they would be living and working close together, even if they were working in different areas.

"There isn't much to do, just a few things to hang in the closet and put away in drawers. But thanks anyway." And she tried to soften the refusal with a smile.

She was not sure just what the girl's problem was, but she seemed to accept the refusal and the smile without taking offense, and Kristen was relieved.

Murmuring a few words, Alicia went out and closed the door softly behind her.

"Well, so much for hands across the border," Kristen sighed and snapped the empty suitcase shut.

CHAPTER 4

Kristen had never known a job could be so fascinating. As history was a special love of hers, she delved into her duties with an alacrity that caused Mrs. Faraday to smile.

One of the upstairs bedrooms had been turned into a library and it was there that Kristen spent most of her mornings. Each day as she met Mrs. Faraday at the breakfast table she was presented with a list of names and places and dates on which she was to find certain information. After eating she would remain with the volumes until lunchtime, often eating a sandwich and continuing her work until it was finished. The afternoons were spent organizing and typing her findings.

She had worked her way through the first couple of weeks with only a scattered hour or two here and there devoted to what Mrs. Faraday so quaintly called "recreational pursuits," but the time had flown by. She was working hard but enjoying herself, so she could not complain. Indeed it was Mrs. Faraday who complained almost daily that she was doing much too much.

"You'll burn yourself out by Christmas time," she prophesied, "and I'll be left with no help at all!"

But she would smile at Kristen's eagerness with understanding; she had been just the same before her eyes had given out on her and had made endless researching impossible.

* * *

Kristen pulled a thick volume from the shelves in the converted bedroom and glanced at its title. Satisfied that this would be the one she would need to complete the study she was doing, she paused to pour herself a cup of coffee from the thermos she kept filled at all times and glanced at her watch. There would be time enough for another hour of work before lunch, but she decided to take out a few moments and enjoy her coffee.

She stood up, stretched her arms out and then up over her head, massaging the cramped muscles at the base of her neck. That was the only drawback about research, she thought with a sigh, you had to remain seated too long. Facts had a wonderful way of hiding themselves in myriads of what she sometimes thought to be unnecessary words.

She had just finished her coffee and had opened the book on the table when the door opened and Alicia walked slowly into the room. Kristen glanced up at her with faint surprise. Ever since their sorry beginning the two girls had seen very little of each other. The house was large, and as Alicia had asserted, their duties were far removed from each other, so their only meetings had been during their meals. Alicia had not sought her out and Kristen had returned the compliment—and anyway she had been so busy she had not thought much of Alicia. So this midmorning visit was unexpected and for Kristen a little puzzling.

Alicia did not speak for a moment but stood contemplating Kristen and the multitudinous stacks of books that were scattered about on the tables and down onto the floor by the chair.

"You have read all of these?" The small brown hand gestured gracefully toward the books and Kristen smiled at the amazement in the girl's voice and the roundness of her dark eyes.

"No, not entirely. You see, you learn to glean out just

what you need at the time and leave the rest until a later time when the need for it arises."

As if she had discovered something very new, Alicia stepped to the table and glanced at the note pad where Kristen was scribbling her findings. She read for a minute and then, unable to make any sense whatever of Kristen's own personal shorthand, she shook her head.

"I do not understand. If there are already books written, then why does Mrs. Faraday just take from those and write another?"

At this Kristen laughed. "She doesn't quite do that," she replied and would have continued, but Alicia turned away with a shrug, murmuring, "It's not important."

So be it, Kristen thought without rancor. Too many people felt much the same way about history for her to get all bent out of shape when this girl did. "How's the art business coming along?" she asked, searching for something to say when Alicia showed no signs of leaving but continued to stand by the table.

Again Alicia shrugged. "We have been waiting for a shipment. One is due to arrive any day now from Saltillo, Mexico." Kristen liked the way she said the words, a smooth, yet lilting sound. "A crate of statues that it is thought were once used in a small mission south of San Antonio."

Interested in the history connected with the statues, Kristen would have liked more information, but Alicia waved all questions aside with one of her fluid gestures which Kristen was learning to watch for. They came often and were most expressive, especially when she was dismissing something as unimportant.

"I did not come up here"—she said this as if she had gone to the outer limits of civilization—"to speak of statues and books. I came to invite you to a party. *Si?*"

Kristen's mouth dropped in astonishment, but she did

not speak, having been left totally bereft of speech from the shock of Alicia's words.

Alicia, fearing a refusal, spoke hurriedly.

"It is only a small party, mostly other students like myself who are studying art at the local colleges. My friend, Rafael, will take us. You would like to go?"

Kristen thought she noted a definite possessive inflection and suspected Rafael was quite likely much more than a friend and opened her mouth to refuse. An evening with Alicia and "friend" did not sound too inviting. But something in the girl's manner seemed to urge her to consent. This was her way of apologizing, she supposed, and paused to reflect.

She had been working quite hard and with very little diversion; there was not much doubt that an evening with this changeable girl and her boyfriend would be diverting, if nothing else.

"All right, Alicia, if you'd really like to have me go and you're sure Rafael won't mind my coming."

She assured Kristen that Rafael would be delighted to have her come along.

Doubting very seriously Rafael's delight, Kristen proceeded that night to dress herself with special care. Even if she were to be a fifth wheel, she would be a presentable one.

With a last quick glance at the mirror she turned and started down the stairs. Even if she had not taken the last look, she would have known her efforts had been a success by the stare she received from the young man who was standing at the foot of the stairs. Smiling back at him, Kristen thought Alicia's choice of young men was excellent.

And a certain amount of charm was present too as he stepped forward and with a flourish reached out and took her hand. He did not shake it but only held it for a long

37

moment, pressed it firmly and then released it slowly and with a great show of reluctance.

At that moment Alicia came into the hallway from the living room and Kristen was almost overwhelmed with a feeling of guilt; with some disgust she felt her color rising, as if she had been caught doing something she should not have done. Alicia turned a stony look toward Rafael and then the dark eyes rested fleetingly on Kristen.

"You have met Kristen Ames, Rafael? Kristen, this is my friend, Rafael Garza. We have known each other for a long while. We are both from Saltillo."

Fearing Rafael might be about to repeat the hand clutching scene, Kristen grasped her handbag tightly, murmured a few words, and then ducked around them both and headed for the door. She hoped fervently that the entire evening was not going to be a series of duckings around Rafael.

Not being familiar with the city, Kristen was unsure exactly where they were going, but Rafael guided the small foreign car, into which Kristen had been doubled up into the rear seat, with great dexterity and abandon. He carried on a running conversation during the course of which he would twist around to include Kristen in the talk, which caused her no end of apprehension. At any other time and in a different set of circumstances Kristen might have been flattered and even pleased by so much masculine attention, but in the midst of all the traffic zipping around them she wished Rafael to Jericho and herself safely back among her books.

After what seemed the longest time they finally pulled up in front of a large modern apartment complex and Rafael nosed neatly into a vacant slot and Kristen breathed a sigh of relief, unfolded herself, and struggled to alight with some semblance of dignity. She refused to contemplate the return drive to the Faraday house. Each problem in its turn.

The party was in full swing and sounds of music and laughter floated down from a second story apartment, causing Kristen to mount the outside stairway with resignation. This had all the signs of being very much like the affairs she had done her best to sidestep during her college years. While not being the least antisocial, she much preferred her gatherings to contain a little less noise, smoke, and people, and when she was ushered into the crowded room, her spirits sank.

It was the usual small room, stuffed to over-capacity with people; the stereo was blaring and everyone was shouting, trying to be heard above it. The small draught of fresh air that came in with them when the door was opened was quickly swallowed up by the smoke. To Kristen it was grim to the extreme.

Then came the constant stream of introductions to disinterested men and women, who were too caught up in their own little cliques to take much time or interest in a new arrival. There were several colleges in San Antonio and there seemed to be representatives of each one present. Aside from several of the familiar looks of appreciation from the male contingent of those gathered, Kristen was soon left to fend for herself.

After a while of struggling for breath in the hazy room she was making her way toward the door and escape when a hand caught her arm. She swung around, prepared to do battle, when to her amazement she found herself gazing up into the face of Clay Courtney. After a speechless moment she found her tongue.

"What on earth are *you* doing here?" she wanted to know. "You turn up in the most unexpected places."

He smiled and she noted again the small wrinkles around his eyes; his eyes were dancing.

"I was looking for you," he told her.

"You were looking for me!" She was aghast. "Here?"

He raised his eyebrows, but he did not speak.

"Whatever gave you the idea I come to things like this?" she asked sharply, gesturing wildly.

His smile broadened. "Well, you're here," he pointed out with unshakable logic.

She frowned and her eyes began to spark. Clay went on hurriedly to explain.

"A friend brought me. He said it was an artsy-craftsy—I think those were the words he used—group, so I—"

"And you considered me artsy-craftsy, is that it?" she yelled, casting a withering glare at the stereo.

Clay reached out suddenly and, taking her arm, ushered her toward the door. "Come on, let's get out of here. We could ruin our vocal chords trying to argue over that racket."

Kristen was stating that she was not arguing as he ushered her through the door. Outside she paused a moment and took a deep breath of fresh air and blinked her smarting eyes and, since Clay was still gripping her arm firmly, followed him down the stairway. He steered her through the parking lot, where he opened the door of a long, white automobile, chrome-trimmed and equipped with all the modern conveniences.

"Another illusion destroyed," she muttered. "No jeep, no pickup?"

"Would it make you feel any better if I said I'd rented it for the evening?"

"Did you?"

"No, Get in."

Kristen climbed in and leaned back against the black upholstery as Clay walked around and slid in under the wheel. When he put the key into the ignition and started the motor, she straightened up quickly.

"But I can't leave!" she cried.

Clay glanced at her in disbelief. "You can't tell me you were enjoying yourself in that mess."

"No, it was a bit too artsy-craftsy even for me," she

said, flashing him a look, "but I should at least tell Alicia and Rafael that I'm—"

"You mean that couple you came in with? They left before we did."

This was a startling piece of news. "Are you sure?"

"Positive. I thought you knew."

Kristen shook her head and leaned back to digest this new development while Clay maneuvered the car from the parking lot out into the street. Now why should Alicia go to all the trouble of taking her to a party where she knew no one and then go off and leave her? As far as they were concerned, she could just as well be back at the Faraday house.

She sat mulling all this over for quite a while and paying scant attention to where they were going until the car stopped suddenly. She sat up and found they were parked to the side of the road on a small rise and the lights of San Antonio lay spread out before them.

She caught her breath. "Isn't it lovely?" she whispered finally, but when Clay switched off the motor, her eyebrows shot up and she eyed him warily.

"Calm down. Your virtue's safe. I'm not going to ravish you. I just wanted to talk and this seemed the best place."

"And just where have I heard that before?" Kristen asked dryly.

Clay laughed. "It did sound true to form, didn't it?"

She turned to face him. "What are you doing in San Antonio anyway? When I met you before, I got the impression that you rarely got off the range, and yet the first time I move out into the social circles, such as they were, there you are."

Clay fished around in his pocket for his cigarettes, offered one to Kristen, who shook her head, and lighted one before answering. In the reflected glow from the cigarette as he pulled at it Kristen saw that the glint of laughter had disappeared from his eyes; his voice had lost its bantering tone.

"I came to San Antonio a day or so ago," he began, "hoping I'd see you, and at the same time hoping I wouldn't. No"—he waved her to silence when she opened her mouth to speak—"let me finish. This may get long and drawn out, but I want you to listen. When I met you a few weeks ago, I was sure then that I didn't want to get involved, so I returned to the ranch determined to forget all about you. And I set about doing it. I can usually control myself or a situation if I set my mind to it."

Silently reflecting, Kristen felt she could believe this.

He went on: "You were too wound up in your career, I told myself, and you'd probably never fit into ranch life and I hadn't planned on falling in love at this particular time. An affair, maybe, but then you didn't seem to be the type that would go for that idea, and aside from that, it didn't hold much appeal for me either—affairs always take up so much of your time and never really lead you anywhere."

At the last part of his statement Kristen straightened up stiffly, her eyes round with indignation. "Well, of all the nerve . . ." she stammered furiously.

"I'm not through," he informed her calmly and resumed as if he were totally unaware of her righteous anger.

"Through some friends I heard about this party tonight. They said I might get a line on you from some of the students. I could have found out where you were through Brian, of course, but I still wasn't sure that was what I really wanted. The party seemed just obscure enough, so I went, certainly not expecting to see you there. But when I did, then I knew that at least we should give it a try and see."

If Kristen had been angry before, now she was incensed.

A long moment went by while she struggled for words and Clay calmly smoked his cigarette.

"So you figure now that your mind is made up what you want to do, that's all that matters? I just fall in step and we move right along? Well, this may be very difficult for someone with your colossal ego to understand, Clay Courtney, but I don't have any intention—"

Clay leaned forward and snubbed out his cigarette in the ashtray and then put a stop to Kristen's tirade by applying the simple method of taking her into his arms and kissing her. A brief struggle ensued, but she soon realized that it was to no avail. She tried passive resistance, but found it difficult to remain passive when being kissed with such fervent expertise.

A moment later, breathlessly, she murmured, "You can't—"

But again her words were stifled as he proved to her that he could, with another kiss that was long, causing her insides to react in a strange sinking manner as he pressed her closer to him with one hand hard at her back and the other moving up the back of her neck and into her hair.

Much later she opened her mouth to speak, but all her protests had been lost somewhere in the muddle of her emotion-ridden thoughts. And his face was so close; his mouth only inches from hers. She closed her mouth without saying a word.

"Now then," he said presently, his voice deep as if it came from deep inside him, "I think I'd better take you home."

His words brought Kristen up with a start. And he smiled.

"You probably won't believe this, but one thing I haven't quite mastered is lovemaking in a car. Much too cramped. I'm used to having lots of room to move."

Kristen watched with stupefaction as he started the car and turned it neatly back toward town.

CHAPTER 5

When the alarm on her small travel clock rang the next morning, Kristen reached out and switched it off but did not get immediately out of bed. She lay for a few moments allowing the last dregs of sleep to dissipate and letting her mind slowly take focus on the new day.

In the far reaches of her sleep-befuddled mind she recalled something had happened to her that had upset her, but she could not recall exactly what it had been. She lay wrapped in a pleasant state of euphoria until the sun shining through the window served to drive away the last remnants of sleep, and as it departed an awareness came to her. And as awareness came so did remembrance of the past evening.

She now recalled fully and with renewed anger and embarrassment what had transpired between herself and Clay. Filled with frustration, she sat up suddenly. She had let him kiss her and she had done precious little to stop him. In fact, she recalled with exasperation and more embarrassment, she had probably let him think she had enjoyed his advances. Once again she had encountered that infuriating man and had come out the loser.

Thoroughly disgusted with herself for not having controlled the situation better, she threw back the covers and climbed out of bed, dressed quickly, and went downstairs for breakfast. As usual she was the first one to the table, and though her humor was not of the best, she greeted

44

Maria Rosa with as much good nature as she could muster and launched into her ham and eggs with an appetite she was far from possessing.

As she gulped down the scalding coffee, she recalled the scene that had taken place on the front porch when Clay, true to his word, had taken her home. They had driven to the Faraday house silently, after Kristen had given him the directions as best she could, and she had opened her door and was making her way up the walk when he had caught up with her. They had mounted the steps in more silence, but when she had reached out to open the door, Clay had placed his hand over hers. He had completely ignored her anger and had spoken in his usual overbearing manner.

"What's your working schedule?" he wanted to know. "And do you have any of the day free?"

Kristen had looked up at him in an amazement that was so complete she found herself answering him.

"I work with Mrs. Faraday in the mornings, if she needs me, and the afternoons are filled with research. I'm not free during the day," she had concluded with satisfaction. Let him do what he could with that, she thought smugly.

His eyebrows had lifted slightly, but he had said nothing. He had put out his hands and took her into his arms as if she would have welcomed his attention, kissed her soundly, lingeringly, and then had murmured something or other about making some arrangements and gone. She had watched him bound down the steps, get into his car, and drive away.

She jabbed her fork into a piece of ham and was chewing it furiously when Alicia came into the room. Kristen's eyes sparkled with hostility as she saw someone upon whom she could vent her anger.

"And just what happened to you and your friend last night?" she demanded as the other girl took her place at the table.

45

Alicia paused as she reached for her fork; she frowned, puzzled. "I do not understand."

Kristen's anger mounted. "Oh, don't play innocent with me! Just why did you and Rafael go off and leave me at that . . . that . . . fiasco?"

Alicia nodded as if she finally understood Kristen's ravings.

"But we did not leave you—it was you who left us." Kristen started to interrupt, but Alicia went calmly on. "Rafael and I left for only a short while, and when we returned, you were not there. We asked about you and were told that you had left with a man."

There was a look in Alicia's eyes that Kristen did not care for, but she decided to let it pass. And there was no chance for further discussion, for Mrs. Faraday at that moment came into the room.

After the morning greetings had been exchanged and Mrs. Faraday had been served, she turned her attention to Alicia.

"Those crates in the front hall, are those the ones we've been expecting from Saltillo?"

Alicia took a sip of her coffee and nodded. "*Si*, Señora, they came this morning. Rafael brought them by for me. I have not opened them yet, for I thought you would be interested in the uncrating of the statues."

Mrs. Faraday smiled, reminding Kristen of a child on Christmas morning anticipating her gifts, and nodded her head with unabashed eagerness. "Yes, we'll see to them directly after we've finished with breakfast. Kristen, I'll leave you to your own devices. No doubt there's still plenty of work to be done in the library."

Kristen said that there was and the sooner she got to it the better. So, excusing herself, she left the two women to their crate opening and went upstairs to the library. Halfway through the morning she thought she heard the front

46

doorbell, but she paid no real attention, determined to keep her mind strictly on her work.

When the doorbell had been answered and Clay was shown into the living room, he was momentarily startled by the mass of clutter that almost obliterated the room. Now what little free space there had been was taken up with crates of differing sizes, which were spilling over with statuary, crockery, excelsior, and wads of newspaper.

Mrs. Faraday, seeing his amazed expression, dismissed Alicia and began an attempt at clearing out enough space so that she might offer the nice-looking young man a place in which to sit, talking all the while, hands fluttering.

"Mr. Courtney, did you say? And you're a friend of Kristen's? Now that's fine, just fine. I'm afraid you've caught me at a bad time—no, no, not bad that you've come, of course!"

At last, through Clay's efforts, a spot was cleared and Mrs. Faraday sat down with him on the couch. "But of course you've come to see Kristen," said a rather breathless Mrs. Faraday, but Clay restrained her before she could summon Maria Rosa.

"As a matter of fact, Mrs. Faraday, I've come to talk with you." When Mrs. Faraday looked faintly surprised, he went on to explain, "I've been doing some thinking, as it comes to my mind that there's more than one method of doing research."

Here Mrs. Faraday inserted a noncommittal, "Oh?"

"Most of the research Kristen's done so far she probably could have done in any city with a library of any size, am I correct?" There was a brief nod. "Shouldn't she be taking advantage of some, shall we call it, on the spot research? She could have someone who knows the city drive her around while she's left free to concentrate entirely on historical points of interest."

A faint smile crinkled about the corners of Mrs. Faraday's mouth; her eyes twinkled. "And I suppose you just happen to have someone in mind who would fit that description?"

"For the furtherance of things literary, I'd be most happy to offer my services," he said with an answering smile.

"Leaving Kristen free to concentrate entirely on historical points of interest," she commented drily.

Here Clay became serious. "I know this research is a business for you, Mrs. Faraday, and that you've hired Kristen to do a job, so I promise not to interfere with her work. She'll get all the facts, you'll have all the information necessary for your book, and I'll . . ."

"Yes," Mrs. Faraday prodded, "and you'll . . . ?"

"Well, let's just say I'll take care of the rest."

Mrs. Faraday smiled and her eyes danced with a mischievous merriment. "Of that, Mr. Courtney, I have little doubt."

Oblivious of the planning and plotting that was going on practically under her feet, Kristen had continued with her work until she heard Mrs. Faraday call to her from the stairway. When she entered the living room, she was startled to find Clay calmly sitting on the couch beside Mrs. Faraday amid the great expanse of clutter. He was inspecting a small statue with apparent interest. When he looked up to see her standing in the doorway, he smiled at her brilliantly and rose to his feet.

"Your employer is a fascinating woman, Kristen," he said, as if it were most natural for him to be there. "She's taken time out of her busy schedule to tell me all about these"—he gestured toward the opened crates at his feet with the statue he was holding—"works of art. Quite interesting—history. Did you know that this"—he held the statue aloft—"is a statue of St. Anthony and it's supposed to be at least one hundred and fifty years old?" He glanced at the figure in his hand and then handed it carefully back to Mrs. Faraday. "He carries his age right well."

Kristen glanced at the woman on the couch to see how she was taking all of this and was dismayed to find that she was smiling as if she were absolutely delighted.

"Mr. Courtney has been telling me that he's a friend of yours and of your sister's," Mrs. Faraday was saying, "and I was so pleased to find you have a friend here in San Antonio. A large city can be a lonely place sometimes if one has no friends there." She gestured to Kristen and began to clear out another spot beside her. "But come, sit down, dear. Mr. Courtney has come up with a most delightful suggestion and I know you're going to agree that it's marvelous."

Doubting this very much, Kristen walked warily into the room and sat down uneasily. She looked past Mrs. Faraday to the opposite end of the couch, where Clay was sitting, and then back to her employer with mounting apprehension.

"A suggestion?" she asked, trying not to sound suspicious.

"Yes, my dear. And I wonder now why I didn't think of it myself. His thought being that it is such a waste to live here amid all these historical spots and for you to be doing all the research from a lot of dusty volumes."

Kristen started to declare that the volumes were not dusty, but restrained herself, casting daggered looks in Clay's direction as best she could around her employer.

"Mr. Courtney is very well acquainted with San Antonio and he's offered, since he has a few days to spend in the city, to drive you around to all these places." She looked at Kristen with a pleased smile. "Now don't you agree that this is a marvelous suggestion? I told him how badly you've wanted to see the city but how you hate to drive in the unfamiliar traffic."

49

Kristen bit back another retort that was forming and struggled to speak civilly in the face of this new and appalling state of affairs.

"I do appreciate your offer, Clay, and as soon as I feel that I've exhausted all the materials available to me, I'll certainly call on you."

Mrs. Faraday waved her hands. "Tut, tut, child! Mr. Courtney has the time now and he might not later. We must take advantage of the present opportunity. The books can wait; they'll certainly be here when you're done. And besides all that, you've been inside much too much, and Mr. Courtney's offer is a heaven-sent opportunity. He's even suggested you start today, and since I'll be tied up with sorting through my new treasures"—she nodded toward the crates where other statuary and bits and pieces could be seen protruding through the excelsior—"this is the ideal time. Now, you come with me, Kristen, and I'll make out a list of places that I want you to see."

Kristen followed in her wake, unable to do anything else, and as Mrs. Faraday moved out into the hall, she heard her say, "And Mr. Courtney has even offered to drive you down to Goliad, if there's time one day soon, and take a picnic lunch and really make a day of it. Doesn't that sound delightful?"

Kristen followed Mrs. Faraday into the small breakfast room with a grim expression and sat down at the table while the older woman proceeded to make notations with a pad and pencil, mumbling thoughtfully to herself.

Due to the combined efforts of Alicia, Rafael, Clay, and now Mrs. Faraday, things were certainly getting out of hand, Kristen thought with wild despair. She was going to have to do something, and that fast.

"Mrs. Faraday," she began, but the other woman silenced her.

"Now don't argue about this, Kristen," she said with a sudden sternness.

Kristen looked at her with surprise. Gone was the sweet, innocent, and somewhat distracted lady of a moment ago. Here instead was a cool, collected, and determined woman.

"I know he's putting one over on you—you don't want to go with him, do you?"

Kristen could only shake her head in wonder.

"Well, more fool you, I say," she answered flatly. "But aside from that, his idea has quite a lot to say for itself. You should take advantage of being able to see as much of this history at first hand as you're able. So what if he's a little arrogant and sure of himself? He certainly has much to his credit."

She purposefully ignored Kristen's widened eyes and turned her attention back to her note pad. She added a few more notes and then handed them to Kristen.

"Here, this should keep your young man busy enough today. I'll work out a better schedule for later." She eyed Kristen for a moment, then added, "And if I were a good deal younger, I wouldn't be sending you, I'd be going myself."

Kristen took the proffered notepaper without a word. After all, what was there to say? She had certainly been outmaneuvered. And then she went up the stairs to her room to change. For just about the first time in her life she had come up against forces that proved stronger than her own and she was left momentarily winded.

Although younger than her sister, Kristen had always been the leader of the two, the more aggressive and dominating. Her aunt and uncle, never very strong personalities, had given Kristen her head, and even her cousin, Martin, had never seen fit to cross her seriously. She had been a leader in her classes all through school and even the boys she had dated had been more apt to let her take the lead and set the pace for their relationships.

And that was why Clay had come as such a shock.

Nothing in her previous experiences had prepared her for such an aggressive and positive force.

For Clay had been brought up in a completely different atmosphere than had Kristen. Instead of being reared by doting foster parents, Clay had lived on a farm where his parents had been so tied up with the struggle of raising crops that they had had scant time to spend on children. So Clay had grown up independent, well able to take care of his own problems. He had worked his way through agricultural college, and now that his ranch was established, he ran it with a firm hand; at an early age he had learned to make decisions quickly and to stick by them.

So when two people, independent and used to taking the lead, and having their lead followed, met, there was sure to be a clash.

After having given her lipstick a swipe across her lips, Kristen set her mouth in a determined line. Clay might believe she had met her match in him, but she did not give up that easily.

Clay was waiting for her at the foot of the stairs and Kristen was relieved that he showed none of the gloating signs of feeling he had come out the victor in their brief struggle of wills. His bland expression seemed to say that nothing exceptional had transpired to give him any reason to feel pride. He had wanted her to go with him and she was going. Just as simple as that.

When she stepped down beside him, Clay smiled with pleasure and held out his hand. "Mrs. Faraday said she had given you a list of places she wanted you to see, so if you'll give it to me . . ."

He paused when he saw Kristen's jaw tightening and the obstinate look come into her eyes. His eyebrows raised questioningly, but Kristen childishly—and she knew full well that she was behaving childishly—held her purse, where the list now rested, firmly in her grip. By holding on to the list it was as if she still held some semblance of command, and right now that seemed terribly important to her.

"You know," Clay said thoughtfully, "it really is surprising how nice you can look when you haven't got that mulish I'm-in-command-around-here look on your face. Trouble is, I don't see you that much without it. Why don't you try relaxing once in a while? You're always wound up so tight."

While Kristen was digesting this, he turned and walked out the front door. Gathering herself together hurriedly, she followed him, congratulating herself on her small victory.

But it seemed the elated feelings were premature; as soon as they were seated in the car, Clay once again put out his hand for the list, explaining as he did—and in a tone that could have been used either for a very small child or for someone with demented faculties—that he would need to know the different places in order to organize the mapping out of their day or they would be running from one side of the town to the other and wasting all their valuable time just fighting traffic.

"Of course," he finished, "if you're familiar enough with San Antonio, then you'll be able to line out the stops in the order that they come in the city."

He leaned back and dug around in his pocket for the key and then inserted it in the ignition; he started the motor and waited to see what she would do. Kristen fingered the clasp on her purse. He had her, of course. As far as she knew, the old Spanish Governor's Palace could be across the street from the Alamo or in the middle of Brackenridge Park. It was silly, and she knew it, to make such a big thing of a small piece of paper, but for Kristen it seemed to represent a shred of independence.

Slowly she opened her purse and silently handed him the list, feeling somewhat as if she were a defeated soldier handing her sword over to the enemy to be broken.

Clay accepted the paper, shaking his head despairingly. "Are you always this bossy and hard to get along with?" he inquired absently as he read over the list. "No wonder you're not married." He took a pencil from the glove compartment and began making notations without looking up.

Kristen was astounded at his words. "*Me* bossy?" She was outraged. "Well, let me tell you that I think you're an arrogant—"

"—and if you don't learn to curb that tongue of yours and learn to smile a little more, *I* might just cry off."

Now she was stung beyond caution. "You probably won't believe this, but I could have had an offer of marriage just in the time since I first met you."

Clay glanced up and eyed her for a moment. "Why shouldn't I believe you? I don't doubt for a minute that you've had men swarming all over you. And this one you just spoke of, no doubt he didn't ask you because he knew he had best wait for your lead. That it wouldn't do to take matters into his own hands. I'm also sure that all those swarming males were more or less of the same stripe, or you wouldn't have had them around. Well, I hate like the devil to tell you this, sweetheart, but following someone else's lead is not what I do best. But we'll make out all right, I think." He grinned suddenly. "You're still fairly young and malleable."

Again he ignored her splutterings and, putting the car into drive, pulled out into the street.

"Now relax and let's try to enjoy our history-seeking tour. Try to forget how you feel about me for the present —I really do have some fine points, which you might discover and learn to like if you'll just let yourself go and quit fighting me at every turn."

CHAPTER 6

It was surprising to Kristen to discover that Clay had a very strong, if not demonstrative, feeling for the old city. When she remarked on this, he laughed.

"I may not go around beating my drum, but I suppose the music's there, somewhere."

They started their sight-seeing at what Clay had remarked was the most logical place for them to begin. "Have you ever been to the Spanish Governor's Palace?" he inquired as he pulled into a parking lot and accepted the ticket from the attendant. When she told him no, he continued: "The palace was, as you no doubt know, the residence of the governor while Texas was under Spanish rule. It may be that the word *palace* is misleading to some. Because of the title people are led to believe they're about to see some moated castle and therefore, are disappointed. And I guess by our standards today, and because of the way the past is sometimes romanticized, it may not look like much when you first set eyes on it. Mind you, I'm not apologizing for it, only explaining. Surrounded as it is on all sides by a foreign—as far as the palace is concerned—and modern civilization, its quaint loveliness is somewhat strangled."

Walking slowly along the crowded sidewalk, Kristen glanced up and Clay's eyes met hers. "Yes?" he asked.

She shook her head. "Nothing, except that someone

listening to you just now would swear that you were the history nut and I was the uninterested bystander."

Clay laughed. "Touché! And heaven forbid! No more lectures, and you have my solemn promise on that."

She stopped in the middle of the sidewalk, paying no attention to the people milling about them. "No, Clay," she protested. "Promise me you'll talk to me just as you were. I enjoy it very much and I want to get your impressions."

"Done," he promised, and pulling her arm through his once again, he propelled her along. "Well, there it is, and if you say, 'Is *that* it?' I swear I'll break your arm!"

Kristen had to admit that at first she was just the least bit disappointed. Built flush to the sidewalk, there was the solid adobe front wall with no ornamentation except for the ornately carved wooden doors and the windows with their wrought iron bars. With the plain white walls and the weathered beams protruding around the top, it appeared—except for the keystone over the doorway displaying the double-headed Spanish eagle and the date 1749 and the small unpretentious plaque declaring that this was, indeed, the palace—to be just another Mexican adobe building.

But after a few moments of study while Clay remained in silence, the first twinge of disappointment had subsided and Kristen was able to appreciate more fully the simple and somewhat austere Spanish charm.

But as they approached the doors, Clay held out a restraining hand.

"Hadn't you better make a few notes about the plaza? I'd hate mighty bad to have you forget something and then have Mrs. Faraday swear I was interfering with your work."

Kristen turned and looked about her at the busy traffic-filled street and frowned.

"I always have a great deal of difficulty doing this—

trying to imagine a bare, dusty road with horses and don-keys pulling carts, women with baskets and water jugs, and a smattering of small *jacales* here and there, when all you can see are paved streets, cars, and multi-storied buildings." Her frown deepened as she concentrated. "Now this was the military plaza, not the main plaza. It was a fairly bloody place—executions and lynchings being regular fare. In those days I imagine the palace was quite impressive."

Clay nodded. "Ready to go in now?"

One of the double doors of the palace was standing open and Kristen could see the small desk in the corner, beyond which she caught a quick glimpse of a curved stairway before Clay ushered her into the next room.

The room they entered was the chapel, complete with ancient images of saints, ornate candlelabra, and a small prie-dieu. Feeling as if she were intruding into some pri-vate place, she strove to walk as quietly as was possible across the uneven flagstone flooring, stepping down as they moved into the dining room. Due to the small win-dows and the walls, which were several feet thick, and despite the warmth of the day outside, it was dark and cool inside and a small fire flickered in the wide fireplace.

They were alone in the room, for it was in the middle of the week and tourists were few. Reaching out, Clay took Kristen's hand, holding it loosely, and she did not attempt to pull it back. It was a quiet, reflective time.

"Are you finding it any easier now?"

Her head swung around from her silent contemplation of the fire. "What? I'm sorry, but I guess I was lost in my thoughts. What did you say?"

Clay smiled down at her and she felt her heart begin to beat strangely. He really did have a most disarming smile.

"I was just wondering if you didn't find it easier now to think of it as it was years ago—the way it was when people lived here, ate their meals here in this room."

Kristen returned his smile. "Much easier. And further-more, I'm not the least bit disappointed in the Governor's Palace."

His grip tightened on the hand he was holding and slowly he lowered his face down to hers. And when his lips touched hers softly, she did not pull back or resist him. When he raised his head, Clay was smiling crookedly.

"I'm not deluding myself that you've surrendered to my fatal charm, but this will do very nicely for a starter. Tell me, are you always this easy to get along with in old Spanish governor's palaces?"

She laughed shakily. "It's the fireplace—they have a certain effect." His kiss had affected her more than she wanted him to see, so moving away hurriedly, she stepped out into the patio.

Surrounded by tall trees and a long archway along one side covered with grape vines, it was almost in soft shade. There were rustic benches constructed of small logs and Kristen trailed her trembling fingers along the roughly hewn bark. She could feel him standing behind her.

"You know," she said into the strained silence, keeping her voice steady with an effort, "you can almost see her sitting here waiting for her lover to come."

Clay's voice came softly at her ear. She could feel the warmth of him as he pressed close to her, his hands resting at her waist. "You're romanticizing. No señorita ever waited for her lover without benefit of her duenna—and duennas had a way of quelling even the most amorous of lovers."

Turning slowly, she looked up into his eyes. "I pity the poor duenna that would have had to deal with you," she said, striving for lightness. "She would have had her hands full."

"It wouldn't have been too difficult—if the señorita was willing."

Left without a reply and not knowing how to deal with

58

the close reality of him, Kristen quickly turned, easing herself from the loose embrace in which he held her, and making her way back through the palace, she stepped back onto the hot, busy sidewalks of a modern, bustling city.

She blinked and Clay, stepping to her side, said, "It's difficult sometimes, isn't it, making the transition—from the past to the present, I mean?"

She looked up at him and was aware, and not for the first time, that he was beginning to understand her much too well and that he was beginning to be too easy to be with and that her response to him was becoming too strong. Before long, if she were not careful, she would find herself following in his wake, obeying his orders, and catering to his whims. If she were not careful, her identity would be lost in his, and she was quite, *quite* sure she did not want that at all.

Nodding briefly, she turned toward the parking lot and, glancing at her watch, announced curtly that they had spent entirely too much time in the palace, she had quite a bit of work to do at home, and would he please take her there. With a lifting of an eyebrow Clay inclined his head in a manner that was very docile, but she was sure she saw amusement in his eyes.

It was late in the afternoon when Clay dropped her at her front door; she went in to find Alicia and Mrs. Faraday just finishing their dinner.

"Oh!" Mrs. Faraday exclaimed, fluttering her hands and asking, "Have you eaten?"

"Yes, we grabbed a sandwich," Kristen answered, pulling a chair from the table and sitting down, "but I'll have coffee with you." After the coffee was poured, Kristen turned to the silent Alicia. "Did you get all the statues unpacked?" When Alicia only nodded, Kristen shrugged and excused herself. She was much too tired to try dragging conversation out of her.

Halfway up the stairs Kristen paused when she heard

59

the telephone ringing; she listened as Maria Rosa struggled with the language barrier and went back down the stairs as the woman motioned to her. She took the receiver with a grim look. If Clay thought he was going to run her life anymore . . .

"Hello." Her voice was short, curt, and then it changed. "Roger! Oh, I am sorry I sounded so short. I've been out most all day and I guess I'm tired."

"I know," Roger replied. "I tried to get you a little earlier, but I didn't do too well. Frankly I couldn't make too much out of what the woman was saying, and she didn't understand me too well either. After a while I gathered you were out and decided I'd best just try again rather than leave a message."

Kristen laughed. It was good to hear his voice. "Maria Rosa's a dear, but she's not too much on English. How have you been?"

"I've missed you, Kris," was his quiet reply.

And something inside her responded to his tone. "And I've missed you," she said, finding after she had said the trite phrase that it was really true. She had missed his quiet, slow ways, his unargumentative and easy-going nature.

"I thought I might come to San Antonio tomorrow in time for dinner," she heard him saying, "if you're not too busy. We could go to dinner and perhaps to a show or a play, anything you'd like."

In her mind's eye she pictured him: Probably he was still at the store, calling from his office, sandy hair brushed across his forehead, brows frowning slightly over gray eyes.

"That would be great," she told him. "I'd really enjoy dinner with you, but let's keep the rest of the evening free, give us time to talk."

The conversation continued briefly. Roger told her news of her family; Kristen described her work, without mentioning Clay. He hung up with the promise that he would be calling again as soon as he arrived in town and Kristen went to her room feeling somehow relieved at just having heard Roger's voice. She found she was actually looking forward to his coming—he had such a calming effect.

Later, after she had spent some time reading and doing some things toward getting ready for the next day, she prepared herself for bed. Switching off the light, she went to the window and sat down to look out into the night, spending the quiet moments just letting her mind slow down and relax.

The night, not totally dark now that her eyes had adjusted, was beautiful, soft, and warm. But instead of relaxing her and making her sleepy, it caused her to become restless. The air, heavily scented from the flowers below, brought its own stimulation.

And moving about in her troubled senses was Clay, stirring her as no one had ever done. Even thoughts of Roger no longer calmed her.

Glancing out into the silver night around her, she sighed heavily. Where had her reality gone, her stability?

But the night contained neither.

CHAPTER 7

Kristen awoke the next morning still filled with the same restlessness, which had not slackened through a night of sleepless tossings.

As she dressed she was drawn again to the window and was again reminded of the garden below. Perhaps there she could relax and regain her balance.

The garden, she found, was lovely, fresh with early morning dew; she walked along a rock pathway, enjoying the smells and sounds around her.

"*Buenos días,* Señorita."

Kristen jerked around, startled. She had thought herself alone. Looking beyond the pathway, she saw Ramon rising to his feet from the midst of a flower bed.

"Good morning, Ramon. I didn't see you there. The flowers are lovely. You've done your work well."

Ramon rubbed his muddy hands along his overalls, gazing about him. "*Sí, gracias Señorita.* I like the flowers —they cannot talk."

Kristen turned her head to keep her smile from him. She had heard Maria Rosa haranguing her husband on more than one occasion and could well understand his feelings for the mute flowers, even if she could not understand why he allowed his wife to do this.

She turned and made her way toward the river; there she found the pathway ended at a small dock, which from the looks of it had not been used in years.

"Ramon," she asked as she walked back to where the man was weeding a flower bed, "does anyone ever use the dock down by the river?"

Ramon glanced back over his shoulder and shook his head. "Not for years, Señorita. It is in bad shape."

She looked at the worn boards, the wood rotting away as the water lapped against it, and then to the banks of the narrow river with the varying shades of green of the plants growing in wild abundance. The morning sun made splashes of brilliance on their shiny leaves.

Resolutely she turned back to the house, determined to conquer this continuing feeling of disquiet which even the early morning beauty of the garden could not dispel. She was going to have her breakfast and retire to the library and she was not going to budge so much as an inch away from the house for the entire day. There was stability in her work and she was determined to attain it.

She had reasoned without Mrs. Faraday.

Kristen was met in the breakfast room by her employer, who handed her, with equal determination, another list. This one was neatly typed and a page long, of places for her to see.

"You're not to allow this perfectly marvelous opportunity," she admonished again when she saw the obstinate look returning to Kristen's eyes, "of being taken around by such an excellent guide to slip through your fingers—our fingers, as it were. I won't allow it. It's absolutely silly to let these beautiful autumn days go on around you while you remain shut up inside in some stuffy room filled with nothing but books."

Kristen was glad to hear that at least she no longer referred to them as "dusty volumes."

"Enough time for reading when you've looked around and the colder weather sets in," she finished and rose from the table. "Alicia and I are still sorting out the statues and things, so I shall be busy with that. What time is Mr. Courtney coming, dear?"

Kristen was striving to remain calm. "He isn't, Mrs. Faraday," she stated quietly but firmly. "That's what I've been trying to tell you. I told him yesterday when he brought me home that I would be much too busy for any more—"

She stopped when she heard the faint peal of the doorbell. Slowly lowering her cup back onto its saucer, she listened as Maria Rosa's footsteps moved softly across the rugs in the hallway to answer the door. She listened to the conversation that ensued and there was no mistaking the cheerful voice that greeted her.

And Kristen discovered she was not in the least surprised; somehow something deep down inside her told her she had expected him to come. She also felt something inside of her beginning to boil.

"Mr. Courtney must have misunderstood you, my dear," Mrs. Faraday was saying in her maddeningly obtuse fashion. "And isn't that fortunate, since you will be able to go with him?" She raised her voice so as to be heard in the hallway: "Will you please show Mr. Courtney in here, Maria Rosa?"

Kristen was aware she was finding it a little difficult to sustain her anger when she saw him coming through the doorway with his smile broad and disarming, falling first upon Mrs. Faraday and then upon herself. He moved into the room with his slow, deliberate gait and took the hand Mrs. Faraday had extended to him, pressing it in his large tanned one.

He then turned to Kristen after having first refused Mrs. Faraday's offer of breakfast. "I'm by habit and by necessity an early riser and I hope I haven't come too early. You failed, or rather I failed to arrange a time for this morning."

64

Kristen's eyes widened at the way in which he chose to ignore completely her statement of the previous evening.

"But I hated to see the morning go to waste," he continued in his easy manner, as if he would find her in total agreement with what he was saying. "It really has all the possibilities of being a great day."

Admitting defeat, Kristen got to her feet. "If you'll please excuse me, I'll go and get my things," she said sharply, her face tinged an angry pink, "for it seems my day has been arranged without benefit of my desires in the matter."

She was further infuriated by Clay's casual announcement that she might need a sweater for the first hour or so.

"Don't you have anything else to do besides run around poking your nose in my business and messing up my life?" she demanded as soon as they were in the car moving into the downtown traffic. "What about your ranch? How can you neglect it? Don't you have branding . . . or something that needs doing?"

"Wrong time of the year for branding," he informed her, maddeningly missing the whole point, "and nothing's being neglected. Shorty's there. He's my partner. You'll like Shorty. He's—"

Kristen shot him a look of surprise and interrupted sharply. "I have no doubt that I would find him a great fellow, *if* I planned on meeting him, *which* I can assure you I do not!" She paused and then asked, "Where are we going?"

She had no idea of the itinerary, for she had turned the list over to Clay without even glancing at it. She had not been about to give him the satisfaction of taking it from her.

"What I should do is drive you back out to that country road where I took you that night after the party," he said after a moment of consideration. "You want kissing badly," he informed her emphatically. "But this isn't the time. I thought we'd go to the Alamo. But, back to what I was saying: You'll like Shorty. He's a good man, but he can't run the ranch alone forever, so I can't stay away too much longer."

"Well, you certainly have my permission to return just any time. Don't, for goodness sake, remain on my account."

Clay was quiet for a time and then quite unexpectedly he burst out laughing, causing her eyebrows to shoot up. "Right now," he told her, still grinning, "I'm thinking that this is all worth it. Man, I sure hope you don't end up disappointing me."

Like most people who have been born in Texas, Kristen, even had she not been the least interested in history, would have been well acquainted with at least some of the happenings at the Alamo. "Remember the Alamo" was not only an old battle cry, it was almost a state of mind.

Clay guided her north along Alamo Street and across the plaza, where they spent a few moments studying the large white cenotaph erected to the memory of the Alamo dead.

"They must have been very brave men," Kristen said finally and Clay shook his head. "You'll need a stronger word than *brave* for those men," he said quietly. "It's one thing to fight when you've got a hope of winning—quite another to stay and fight when there's no hope and you know it. But in doing so, they gave Sam Houston the time he needed, so they didn't die in vain."

Kristen took another long look at the cenotaph and then turned to Clay. She started to speak, but he took her arm and walked across toward the old stone mission. He waited patiently while she found just the right spot on the smooth flagstones to stand and take a picture; he steadfastly refused to stand in the entrance with what he called an idiotic tourist smile plastered across his face while she snapped the picture.

"Then don't smile," she told him, but he stood his ground and shook his head.

"Go ahead and take your pictures. We're wasting time."

She wrinkled her nose at him disapprovingly and snapped her picture. "Isn't the carving lovely?" she commented as they walked toward the entrance, struggling to walk, look about her, and get her camera back into the leather carrying case all at the same time, and managing all three fairly poorly.

"Here, let me have that," Clay said with some exasperation, taking the camera from her and slipping the offender back into the case. "I'll carry the thing around and let everyone think I'm one of those picture-taking tourists."

Adjusting the leather strap over his shoulder, he then agreed that the carving was lovely and pointed out the empty niches where statues of saints had once stood, commenting that perhaps Mrs. Faraday just might find the missing saints and restore them to their pedestals. He showed her the ornate and intricate patterns of the carvings in the archway over the double doors, the four pillars with their twisted effect placed flush against the front of the building, the beauty of the weather-worn stone, glowing golden in the morning sunshine.

They entered the large, high-ceilinged room where sounds echoed and people crowded around the many display cases. The fact that this was not the normal tourist season had not thinned the crowd appreciably and Kristen was unable to put herself back in time here amid all the noise and confusion as she had in the undisturbed quiet of the Governor's Palace.

"There's a garden out here," Clay explained after they had made their way through the building and were standing near the back. "And there's an arcade where it's usually not so crowded."

They walked in the garden, where even this late in the season flowers were still in brilliant bloom. The sun shining through the trees was softly warm; it was quiet walking beneath the shadowy arcade. They were alone, except for an occasional couple; the sounds of the city traffic were somehow muffled and remote.

Reaching an isolated spot free of sightseers, Clay released the hand he had been holding and slipped his arm around her waist. Unconscious of her action when he turned her around to face him, she automatically lifted her face for his kiss. Because people were apt to turn up at any moment, the kiss was not long, but nevertheless Kristen could feel the undercurrents moving beneath its surface, telling her that his kisses would become more demanding.

With the thought of these demands something inside her began to contract and to harden. She felt almost a sense of panic. None of the men she had known before had ever demanded anything of her, not even love. She had never allowed this to happen.

Now the tension returned and moved through her body and Clay, sensing this, lifted his head and looked down at her.

"You're drawn up tight again," he said, shaking his head. "What did I do wrong? I thought I was handling everything quite well."

He released her slowly; the mood was broken and there was no need to try to hold on to it. Kristen walked along beside him at a brisk pace, not looking in his direction.

"Oh, you needn't worry," she assured him, striving to keep her voice cool and steady, detached, "your technique was admirable. It just happens that it doesn't appeal to me."

"Yes," he agreed promptly, "I could tell that."

Kristen glanced at him suspiciously, wondering if he

knew just how much his kiss had affected her, but his face was devoid of expression. She started to speak, but he cut off her words.

"Are you hungry?"

Kristen stopped dead in her tracks. "What?" She gaped at him, positive she had misunderstood him.

"I said, are you hungry?" He glanced at his watch. "I know it may seem early, but at home I would've been up for hours and had breakfast a long time gone. Even away I can't break the habit of an early lunch and there's a place down on the river where we can eat if you don't think it's too early."

Astounded by the abrupt change, Kristen mumbled something she feared was unintelligible and then found herself falling into step as he led her out of the arcade and down the busy street to the first steps leading down to the river.

She walked with her brain in whirl. Clay, with his mercurial changes, kept throwing her miserably off stride. Just when she was positive she knew exactly how he would act or react, he would pull something which left her bereft of thought and unsure of action.

Thus it was she found herself on her way to lunch by the river when she had fully intended to be on her way back to the calm surety of her research and out of this muddled indecision.

Kristen was finding that a large measure of San Antonio's charm rested in the way one moved from the past to the present just by walking through a doorway. Now she was discovering a new and different manner of divorcing herself from the city—by means of descending a few steps and leaving all the hurry behind to walk the quiet, unhurried banks of the river.

The San Antonio River wound its way through the city at a lower level, meandering along beneath the streets. On either side of the narrow, dark-green waters of the river were flagstone walks curved to fit the turns made by the water. All about were beds filled with flowers, plants with broad, shiny leaves, bushes of all sizes, some heavy with blossoms; fountains splashed noisily and tall trees spread their branches out low over the water.

To further add to the charm there were occasional shops spilling out their wares in brilliant colors, and sidewalk cafés with dark, swarthily handsome waiters between the small tables covered with crisp, gaily checkered cloths. Every now and then a paddleboat could be seen churning the smooth waters as it made its ponderous way, propelled by laughing children and adults alike.

The whole effect was one of complete relaxation with a Continental flavor that suggested the postponement of all problems to that never attainable *mañana*. Kristen reveled in it and Clay, glancing down at her averted face, smiled. And when she turned to him suddenly, she was caught by the look of tenderness that she found there.

"Pretty, isn't it?" he said quickly and the fleeting glimpse of tenderness was gone. *You're going to have to watch yourself,* he said to himself sternly, *or she'll have you in tow and you'll be just another poor wretch following in her wake. And she'll have lost what might prove to be the only chance she'll ever have to be the woman she can be— warm and loving and giving.*

Kristen nodded, slightly puzzled. "Very pretty," she agreed vaguely, her mind now occupied with the man beside her.

"It hasn't always been this way, you know," he went on in an offhanded way, purposely ignoring her look. "Oh, it was well enough in the daytime, but after dark it used to be poorly lighted, and although quite romantic, you could darn well get your head bashed in for your trouble."

"What price romance?" Kristen inserted with a smile.

"Exactly. But now that's all changed. There's one place in particular I've enjoyed and I think you'd probably enjoy it too. If you'd like, I could pick you up tonight around nine and we'll drop in. There's no food served, only coffee and drinks, but there's a Dixieland band that's really great, if you like that kind of music."

The invitation had been thrown more or less casually into the conversation, and when Kristen assured him she did enjoy Dixieland very much while still fumbling for an answer, Clay took this for an acceptance and said: "Good. I'll be around to pick you up at nine."

Finally Kristen found her words. "I'm sorry, Clay, but I can't tonight." She hesitated and then added, "I have other plans."

He turned and looked down at her; she knew it had sounded as if the excuse had been made up on the spot.

"A man I know," she went on quickly to explain, "from home called last evening and he's coming in to take me to dinner."

She knew he believed her; she could see it in his eyes. "Who is he?"

"His name is Roger Franklin," she began hesitatingly. She had never done this before, describe one man she knew to another. "I've known him for years." She was floundering. "A close friend . . . of the family. He works with my uncle, or rather he's buying the store from my uncle."

She stopped; he looked at her for a moment.

"He sounds like a fine fellow." And Kristen could detect no sarcasm. He added, "We'll make it another time."

And he took her arm, motioning her toward a small grouping of tables near the water's edge.

"Did you know the river flows just behind Mrs. Faraday's house?" she said, searching for conversation. "I spent some time out in the garden this morning talking to Ramon."

His eyebrows raised questioningly. "And who's Ramon?"

71

"Maria Rosa's husband. He prefers flowers. It seems they're quieter."

When Clay pulled up to the curb almost an hour later, Kristen took a quick guilty look at her watch, sighed and heard Clay laugh.

"All right for you," she flung at him, "but many more days like today and I'll probably find myself without a job."

From all appearances she decided he did not think this possibility too earthshaking. She reached out to open the door, but Clay leaned across her and put a quick hand over hers, stopping her.

"Wait just another minute, Kristen." He was suddenly serious. "For me it's been a wonderful day—and for you too, if you'll only admit it. There were moments when you were warm and responsive and that's the woman I'm interested in. The woman I want—and make no mistake, sweetheart, I want her badly."

His arm dropped from the seat behind her to her shoulders and pressed her to him firmly. His kiss was calculated to stir her to the point of dispelling all else and bringing the warmth once again to the surface. And for a long, delicious moment he succeeded. When he raised his head, she looked at him without speaking, and he noted with satisfaction that her breath was coming faster; her breasts were rising and falling rapidly.

He left her at the door with a parting admonition. "I'll see you at another time."

CHAPTER 8

Kristen went in to discover, by way of Maria Rosa's halt-ing English, that Mrs. Faraday had gone to a meeting, and she could see Alicia in the living room walking aimlessly about, checking on the various statuary, making notes on a pad. When Kristen stepped into the room, Alicia, hear-ing her enter, looked up from her work. She stared at Kristen for a moment and then spoke.

"What are you doing here?"

Taken aback by this unexpected greeting, Kristen frowned, saying, "I live here, remember?"

Alicia put her pen aside. "Mrs. Faraday said you were out."

Kristen watched her, trying to speak lightly. "Mrs. Faraday was right—I was out. But now I'm in, but not for long. I've got to get dressed for a dinner date." She found now that she was rattling—sometimes Alicia just flat made her nervous. "A friend from home is visiting—tak-ing me out."

The telephone rang suddenly and she was not sure who jumped higher, herself or Alicia. Both moved for the door, but Maria Rosa was there first. It turned out to be Roger; he would pick her up in an hour, so Kristen went hurried-ly up the stairs to bathe and change.

Roger arrived promptly and Kristen greeted him warm-ly, smiling as he took her hands and kissed her lightly.

73

They were almost the same height and she could very nearly stand eye to eye with him.

"It's marvelous, Roger, for you to come all the way here to see me. It's like going home."

To Roger's question of where she preferred to eat, she told him truthfully that she had no idea about any of the restaurants and would have to leave it to him. He responded by pulling into the parking lot of a large colonial structure, quite like nothing she had seen in San Antonio, and found herself being ushered into a dining room most elegantly done in white and gold with touches of red velvet.

"I hope," she said over her shoulder as Roger helped her with her chair, "that I'm dressed well enough for this."

She saw him smile. "You're fine. By far the loveliest woman in the room."

Glancing around, Kristen felt this quite likely to be true—due largely to the fact that there were precious few tables filled. But despite the stiff surroundings, the austere feel of the place, she relaxed and began to discuss with Roger the dinner they were about to order. It was so simple to fall right back into the pattern that had been established between them through the years, the comfort of the old glove, the easy fit with no demands.

After their order had been taken, Kristen asked, "And how's everything going at the store?"

But strangely Roger did not respond as he usually did; he answered her question but with none of his usual excitement. When he had finished, he paused and then said, "Are you happy here, Kristen? Do you like your work?"

This time Roger had asked the magic question and she responded as he had not. "I am tremendously happy, Roger, and I didn't know I could enjoy working so much. Mrs. Faraday is a wonder and we understand each other, which is great. And we work very well together. She's a very stimulating woman."

She went on until she realized she was doing all the talking and then leaned forward to place her hand on his.

"Please forgive me, Roger, for going on like that," she told him tritely. "I guess you just punched the right button."

In an easy movement he turned his hand and grasped hers, pressing it gently; he would have spoken, but the waiter appeared and conversation stopped as dinner was served.

Later, driving about the city, Kristen, although still none too familiar with her surroundings and especially at night, strove to recognize points of interest. She was failing miserably when suddenly she pointed excitedly upward out of her window.

"Look! Something I honestly recognize! It's the Tower of the Americas. You remember, Roger, from the Hemisfair. There's a restaurant on the top and I think there's an observation platform. Let's go up there and see. San Antonio must be lovely from there after dark with all the lights."

Minutes later, after a rather startling ride in a glass-fronted, outside elevator, they were over six hundred feet above the ground, with San Antonio sparkling at their feet.

"Glorious!" Kristen murmured as the wind whipped her hair about her face.

Roger smiled at her, took her hand, and they walked slowly around the top of the tower, meeting from time to time other couples equally intent on the view, or upon each other.

"Kristen," Roger said, his face near hers to make himself heard over the wind. When she turned to face him, his lips touched hers and held. "Come home with me," he whispered.

"I can't, Roger," she answered softly, "not just yet. There's so much I have to do."

His arms tightened around her while his voice strove for lightness. "At least you didn't say not ever. I guess I'll just have to wait until you're ready. Just remember, I miss you terribly."

She smiled at him, grateful for his understanding, for his not pushing her.

It was cool in the night wind and after a while Roger went inside in search of coffee, while Kristen stood looking down, her gaze intent on the scene below her. San Antonio was spread all around her like jewels sparkling on black velvet, all lying at her feet. Hers to dip into with both hands, to grasp and to hold. And she wanted to do this, to reach out and embrace all of it.

It was all so exhilarating. She found herself shivering, whether from excitement or the chill of the strong night wind she did not know.

Looking around, she saw Roger coming, with two cups of coffee steaming in his hands; she accepted one gratefully, and then silently they continued their walk around the tower. Both were lost in their own thoughts, Kristen thrilled with the joy that was San Antonio, Roger wondering how he would ever get her away and back home again.

It was late when he brought her home and he refused her offer to come in, saying he should get back to the motel and to bed, for he would be leaving early in the morning in order to get back to the store.

He took her into his arms, his kiss long and lingering, as if he were reluctant to let her go.

"It was a wonderful evening, Roger," Kristen said. "Thank you for coming."

He smiled at her. "I'll call you soon," he promised.

She went up to her room and to bed with a relaxed satisfaction she had not felt for some time.

CHAPTER 9

Kristen worked steadily the next day and with no interruptions. Roger had left so early he had not called. Purposefully she kept her thoughts riveted on her work and steadfastly away from Clay, for there lay confusion.

It was late in the afternoon when he called.

"I'm offering the same program as last night," he told her. "If you're interested."

It was on her tongue to refuse; she had fully intended to say no and had actually rehearsed how she would say it if he called. She surprised herself by answering, "Same time?"

"Nine o'clock."

Around seven Kristen went into the kitchen to fix herself a quick snack. Clay had warned her that supper would be late and she was searching through the refrigerator when Alicia walked into the kitchen. Kristen glanced up, spoke, and then resumed her searching, not expecting Alicia to stay around; she never did for long.

She told herself she had tried to be friendly but none of her attempts had met with more than nominal success. Alicia did her work, went out on occasion with Rafael, and kept to herself. So Kristen had taken the hint. But now, surprisingly, Alicia showed no signs of leaving but pulled out a chair and watched as Kristen made herself a sandwich.

"Want one?" Kristen asked, holding up a slice of bread, but the girl shook her head.

"No," she replied, "I will eat with the señora."

Kristen noticed Alicia was watching her with open curiosity and after a time of consideration Alicia spoke again.

"Why do you eat now? Why do you not wait for the señora?"

Kristen hesitated before answering, picking up a knife and beginning to slice off a thick piece of ham.

"I'm going out for a late supper," Kristen informed her, telling as few of the details as was possible, "and I'm just fortifying to slow down any possible stomach rumbles." She frowned at the answering glint in Alicia's eyes.

"The man who took you out last night. You are going out with him again tonight?"

Kristen shook her head. "No, not that man."

"Oh, the man you found at the party."

Kristen put down the knife. "He didn't just pick me up at that party, you know," she answered tartly. "He's an old friend"—she paused—"of my sister and her husband." She regretted those last words, for they were added without truth and were therefore lacking in conviction. Turning from Alicia's knowing look, she proceeded to pour herself a glass of milk.

"It is good you have found a friend," Alicia commented. "It is not good for a woman to spend so much time alone."

Then she undulated—that was the only word Kristen could think of which properly described the fluid movements—toward the door, but as she walked through, she tossed a departing remark back across her shoulder: "Your friend, he is very much man,"—thus leaving Kristen to seethe over the implication that he was a lot more man than Alicia thought Kristen was woman enough to handle.

It was with a certain amount of defiance that Kristen

dressed for her date with Clay. Goaded on by Alicia's stinging aspersions on her womanhood, she took special pains to make herself attractive.

Was it possible that she gave the appearance of being a woman unable to hold her own against a man such as Clay, or was Alicia just trying to cause trouble? It was true, of course, that Clay was not the type she had dated in the past, but that had not been because she had been afraid to date a man she could not dominate. She was not that sort of woman. Or was she?

Her thoughts spun on in this manner until she finished dressing, but when she stood before her mirror, she was pleased to find that despite all she had come out looking fairly well. Her dark hair was curled softly about her face and for some reason her blue eyes, nestled in their black lashes, were shining brilliantly.

When she walked into the living room, she felt strangely elated and somehow vindicated when she saw the look of approval and appreciation in Clay's eyes. He stepped forward to meet her and took her hand in his; his golden eyes glinted.

"Just what I'd hoped for but hadn't allowed myself to expect," he murmured softly. "You look fantastic."

"Mr. Courtney. I thought I heard the doorbell. How delightful to see you again."

Kristen jumped and stepped back hurriedly. Clay grinned and took Mrs. Faraday's outstretched hand without relinquishing his hold on Kristen's. Mrs. Faraday turned to Kristen with a happy smile.

"How very nice you look, my dear. That dress is perfect on you, don't you think so, Mr. Courtney?" Not waiting for Clay to answer, she hurried on. "And you're going out strictly for pleasure, I see. Well, that's just wonderful, wonderful. And it's just what she needs to do, so I won't detain you another minute. See that she relaxes, Mr. Courtney. Kristen is apt to take her work much too seriously for someone as young and pretty as she is. Good night, my dears, and have a lovely time."

"The only thing she didn't do was throw kisses," Kristen commented dryly as Clay helped her into the car.

"She likes you very much and only wants to see you happy."

"Oh?" Kristen kept her voice light. "And what do you think her opinion of happiness is?"

His eyes held hers. "Happiness, in her opinion, is a man who loves you," he murmured before he closed the door.

The nightclub, with its entrance facing the river, was small, but as the evening was still early, they had no trouble getting the table Clay wanted, secluded in a corner. The waitress came, took their order, and as conversation was almost an impossibility, they settled back to listen to the loud, brassy sound of the Dixieland band. As she listened and sipped her coffee, Kristen looked around. There were only about twenty tables in the place and only half of them were filled; the room was dimly lighted by small hurricane lamps hanging along walls that had been papered a deep red. The waitresses were clad in short, full-skirted cancan costumes complete with red lace garters; they moved easily in and out among the tables with an occasional flounce revealing a flash of red ruffles and black tights.

There was hardly a pause between the musical numbers, so talk had been ruled out, and as Kristen studied Clay covertly she discovered she was somewhat nettled by his complete absorption in the music and his complete obliviousness of her. She made a concentrated effort to listen to the band, which she knew was really good, and to forget about him as he had forgotten her, but for some perverse reason she could not.

Why should she suddenly want those eyes looking at her? Up until now she had thought him arrogant and had scorned all his attentions, but at the moment she actually wanted him to turn to her, to be as aware of her as she was of him. She wondered suddenly if he was angry because she had gone out with Roger. But he didn't seem angry, only absorbed in the music.

"Is something wrong, Kristen?"

His words, his head now bent to hers, caused her to start and her heart to pound. His chair was next to hers and he had leaned toward her, placing his arm across the back of her chair. Through the dim light his eyes sought to search hers.

"Is the music too loud?" he asked when she did not speak. "Is it giving you a headache? I love it and I get so wound up in it that I don't always notice the volume."

Kristen smiled, rather ruefully, she was afraid. "Yes, I could see you were enjoying it."

Once again his eyes searched hers and she could feel him reading her thoughts; she knew he was sensing her feelings. She also knew that her face was coloring; she could feel the warmth.

When he spoke, his words were measured, as if in some way they held a warning. "Do you want to leave?"

She could not drop her eyes. She tried, but they seemed to be fastened to his. "But the music," she faltered, "you were enjoying it so much and I hate to spoil—"

Clay got to his feet and put his hand out to help Kristen to hers. "Devil take the music," he muttered and started guiding her toward the entrance. They were stepping out the door when they were stopped suddenly by someone calling from within the club.

"Clay! Clay Courtney!"

It was a woman's voice and Kristen swung around to see a tall blonde walking toward them in long, leggy strides.

"Clay! I thought that was you!"

She walked up, held out both hands, and Clay took

them in his. To Kristen's startled amazement he then leaned forward to plant a kiss on the upturned cheek.

"Whatever are you doing in San Antonio?" the blonde went on, smiling brilliantly up into his face.

She was not exactly beautiful, but she was a very attractive woman all the same, Kristen conceded grudgingly, with her blond hair—naturally blond at that—flowing to her shoulders, her skin tanned and glowing. And she was simply overflowing with joy at having run into Clay.

"And just why haven't you called," she was demanding, "and let someone know you're around?"

The brief pleasure Kristen experienced over the fact that he had not called was dispelled by Clay's words.

"But I did call, Honey, and if you'll slow down the questions for a minute"—he laughed—"I'll try my best to come up with some answers."

At his use of the endearment, however casual, Kristen felt something harden inside of her, leaving her suddenly cold.

"I had some business to attend to, so I came in for a few days—and I did try to call you several times, but as usual you were out somewhere."

The coldness began to solidify. The blonde was laughing in a most friendly and intimate way, or so it seemed to Kristen, who remained on the outside of the conversation looking in.

"Your story!" the blonde was accusing him. Then she glanced quickly around. "But where's Shorty?"

Clay's grin broadened. "I wondered when you'd get around to asking about him. He's back at the ranch keeping things together. I planned to be gone too long for both of us to come away together. I have a small problem I'm working on." Kristen realized he was describing her.

The blonde cocked her head prettily. "I hate to be inquisitive, but why are you here? There's not a horse or cattle show for weeks."

82

Clay shook his head in mock despair. "In case your mother hasn't told you, Honey, there's more to life than horses."

Kristen felt as if she were turning into ice-cold stone. But why should she feel this way? Clay certainly had not gotten all bent out of shape when he heard about her date with Roger. But then he hadn't had to stand and face Roger, and watch him smile prettily, and hear her call him honey, she thought, trying to look composed.

Then with a sudden movement Clay reached out, grasped her hand, and pulled her next to him. "Honey, I want you to meet someone. Kristen Ames—Honey Moore."

Kristen smiled weakly. Why would anyone want to give their child a name like Honey? It could lead to nothing but confusion. She mumbled a few words she hoped were correct and polite and tried to broaden her smile to match Honey's.

There were a few more minutes of casual conversation during which Kristen learned that Honey and her parents owned a ranch just outside of San Antonio near the town of Helotes and that she had known Clay forever. The talk was short, but not too short for Clay to promise to drive out to look over some horse Honey had just bought and wanted him to see. He turned down the invitation to join her party and they said good night and stepped outside.

The cool night air was refreshing after the tightness of the club and the quiet was almost overpowering. They walked a few paces down the river walk before Kristen blurted out: "I've often wondered how you came to know San Antonio so well, but it appears you spend quite a bit of time here—at least Honey seems to know you quite well."

She saw his eyebrows move upward and was furious with herself. *No wonder he looks like that,* she told herself with disgust. *You sounded exactly as if you were jealous.*

But Clay did not speak until they came to a secluded bench where he sat down, pulling her down beside him.

"You're not upset about Honey, are you? There's nothing between us and there never has been—not like that. I'm sure she'd much rather be with Shorty."

Kristen's face, close to his, looked disbelieving. "No way can you make me believe a statuesque blonde like that can be interested in someone called Shorty."

Clay spoke as if the subject had completely lost his interest, as if his mind were on other things. "Shorty is just a nickname for a guy who's six foot six and weighs about two-thirty, and is great-looking if you can judge by the females he's continually having to fight off." Then his voice became softer, deeper. "Forget about Honey," he repeated, his mouth caressing her neck, moving up to play softly about her lips, "and think about you and me—as you were before we ran into her." He felt her stiffen. "And don't start denying it, sweetheart. I could see it in your eyes. You were wanting me, and like a fool, I was intent on the music."

One hand pressed at her back while the other moved in her hair. His mouth was warm on hers, making her reel; her breath grew more uneven. Clay loosened his grip on her slowly; he looked at her, and though his eyes were warm, his voice was quiet.

"This is not the place for this," he ground out between his teeth. "In another minute a cop will be around tapping me on the shoulder." He was frowning now, and when he spoke, he sounded resigned. "Looks like you win another round. Wouldn't you just know that you'd come to life in a place like this, where you're unattainable? But by the time we walk to the car, unless I stop and kiss you every two feet, your usual cool, detached other-self will have returned. Come on, honey, and I'll take you home before my resolve runs out."

84

CHAPTER 10

Kristen did not see Clay the next day, or hear from him, nor did Roger call. One minute she would think of Roger having forgotten her completely over something as mundane as a store; also she went about her work followed by visions of Clay and Honey riding the range together, her blond hair flowing and her smile brilliant.

Her mind was plagued by troublesome questions. What did Clay think about the way she had acted last night? Had he misunderstood—or had he understood all too well? And what had possessed her to act in such a way? And why didn't he call?

Her work suffered; she could not keep her mind on her books and her thoughts were a shambles. She saw Mrs. Faraday at supper and was relieved to find the lady was expecting another crate of goodies any day now and was so excited she did not think to ask about Clay and why he had not been around that day. Alicia too remained silent, but her eyes spoke—Kristen was glad she could not understand the language.

Excusing herself by saying she had a slight headache, Kristen started toward her room and Mrs. Faraday came to herself long enough to give Kristen a long thoughtful look.

"You don't look too well, my dear. You've probably been doing too much reading. Perhaps Mr. Courtney will be able to come around tomorrow and you'll have a chance to get out for a while. Or maybe the other nice gentleman."

Kristen forbore telling her that this had been the first day she had spent inside for a while, and that the other nice gentleman was miles away and had obviously forgotten her, mumbled something, and escaped in the direction of her room.

She went to bed early, but sleep eluded her. She spent what seemed like hours tossing before she finally, from pure exhaustion, fell asleep. Having gotten to sleep later than usual, Kristen was sleeping soundly when she heard a soft tapping at her bedroom door. She roused up instantly, though she was still in a fog of sleep.

"Yes?" she called out, glancing toward the window to see if perhaps she had overslept, but it was still dark outside. "Who is it? Mrs. Faraday?"

Switching on the lamp by the bed, she saw by the clock that it was only a little after five. Fearing something was wrong, she was beginning to scramble out of bed and groping for her robe when the door opened to reveal Maria Rosa wrapped in a voluminous bathrobe, her eyes still swollen from sleep.

"Pardon, Señorita, but the Señor Courtney," she said haltingly, "he has come. He sends me to say for you to dress in the slacks"—she said the strange word hesitatingly—"and to come downstairs pronto. He will wait."

Fully awake now, Kristen began to bristle with anger. And just who did he think he was? He doesn't come around or call all day and then shows up at this hour, getting people out of bed, issuing orders, and expecting them to be carried out without question. Well, he would have a long wait, indeed!

"Maria Rosa, you go back downstairs and tell the Señor Courtney that I don't intend to—"

She was interrupted by a familiar voice coming from the darkness behind Maria Rosa. "You'd better do as the

Señor Courtney tells you, my love, quickly and quietly, or I shall be forced to come in and assist. I'll wait for what I consider to be time enough and then in I come. It's your decision."

The door closed and Kristen, not afraid he would really make good on his threat, but knowing he could end up getting everyone out of bed and causing untold confusion, climbed from hers and began to dress. She was drawn up short by his voice coming through the door.

"And wear flat shoes," came the further orders.

Yes, sir! she thought, mentally saluting. She ran a comb through her tousled hair, gave her nose a cursory dab of powder, and swiped on a quick application of lipstick. He was standing, waiting for her, at the bottom of the stairway and he looked her over with satisfaction.

"Slacks, sweater, flat shoes—and all in under thirty minutes. I adore a woman who can do that and still come out looking great."

Kristen glared at him. "Your praise makes this all worthwhile," she said caustically. "Now, would you mind telling me what this madness is all about?"

But he shook his head. "Not until we're in the car and you can't back out. Besides we'll wake everyone if we talk here. I've told Maria Rosa what to tell Mrs. Faraday, so let's go." He grabbed her hand and started toward the door and then stopped. "Got your notebook?" Speechless by now, Kristen only nodded and indicated her purse. "Good, then let's go."

"Now I demand to know what this is all about," Kristen stated emphatically once they were seated in the car.

"We're going to Goliad for the day," he said easily, as he started the car. "You can take notes like crazy, have a glorious day, and not feel the least bit guilty. Maria Rosa will tell Mrs. Faraday where we've gone and she'll think it's a grand idea. I even had the restaurant pack us a lunch, so you see, all's well."

Kristen sank back and cast her eyes toward heaven. "Poor Maria Rosa. She doubtless didn't understand five words that you told her—so she probably thinks we're eloping, if not something worse."

Clay laughed. "Now that's not a bad idea, but I left a note for Mrs. Faraday just in case the language barrier created a problem."

"Would you mind telling me just how you managed to get Maria Rosa up without rousing the entire household?"

"Not at all. I used the age-old method. I tossed a few rocks—small ones, of course. And you know, it works! I wasn't sure which window was yours, but I figured the one at the top had to be Maria Rosa's."

Kristen shook her head in despair. "She probably thinks you're *loco* in the *cabeza* and need to be humored. That's a term she applies to Ramon from time to time and I'm very sure she'll be applying it to you quite frequently after this morning."

They rode along in silence for a time while Clay searched for the right turn off the freeway, explaining that he had made the wrong turn once and had almost ended up in Laredo."

"Come to think of it," he added, "that might not be a bad idea."

Not liking the tone of his voice, Kristen asked warily, "What might not be a bad idea?"

"Going to Laredo. It's right on the Mexican border and I've never eloped to Mexico before. What about you?"

"Sorry to disappoint you, but Goliad is as far as I'm paid up on this trip. And don't sound so confounded cheerful. I warn you, when I get fully awake, I'm going to be madder than—"

"Watch your language. There's coffee in a thermos at your feet and some doughnuts if you're hungry."

Kristen poured herself some coffee, offered a cup to

Clay, and when he shook his head, she sipped her own gratefully, allowing it to wash away the last dregs of sleep.

After they had made their turn from the freeway and were moving south along the highway, Kristen stole a quick glance at Clay, wondering if he would mention what he had done and where he had been all day yesterday. She decided he probably would not. After all, she had no claim whatever on his time, so why should he account for himself to her? Still she burned to know but would not give him the satisfaction of letting him know it.

Then, as if he had known exactly what she had been thinking, he said, "Sorry about yesterday, but I got tied up."

"Oh?" she said in what she hoped was a totally disinterested, noncommittal tone of voice.

"I went out to Helotes to see the Moores and one thing led to another."

I can just imagine, she thought, but remained silent.

"The Moores, as you've heard, have been good friends of mine for years. They raise mostly horses on their ranch, some cattle of course, but mostly horses and some really fine ones. I have some mares that'll be coming in season soon and I wanted to see about taking one of their studs down when I go back."

Kristen finished her coffee and replaced the cup. "How romantic," she said dryly.

Clay laughed loudly, reaching out as he did, grasping her wrist and pulling her over to his side of the car. He circled her waist with his arm, and slipping his hand around her thigh, he tucked her snugly against him.

Kristen stiffened and started to pull away. "But you can't drive like this!" she told him.

"Oh, yes I can," he assured her firmly, "but if it's going to take two hands to corral you, I sure as blazes can't—I'll need at least one for the wheel."

She sighed and relaxed. "Did it ever occur to you that you might ask me once in a while?"

His hand was still resting on her thigh, but she decided to ignore it.

"Ask you what?" he inquired.

"Ask me what I'd like to do."

He gave her a sidelong glance. "It's okay by me. What did you have in mind?"

"You know very well what I mean," she went on doggedly. "You never ask me—you tell me. Take this trip to Goliad, for instance. Why didn't you just ask me if I'd like to go to Goliad instead of going through all this rock tossing at windows and all the rest?"

"For the simple reason," he explained, "that you'd have said no and then you'd have set about throwing obstacles in my path by the gross. Then I would have had to bring in Mrs. Faraday to run interference and all that would have taken a lot of time. It's much easier my way. See, we're on our way with no obstacles, no Mrs. Faraday, and all that time saved."

After a long pause Kristen asked offhandedly, "When are you going back to the Moores' to pick up the horse?"

He shrugged. "I'm in no hurry—and what's more important, neither are the mares. But I've got to go out again and help Honey with that horse she bought. It's a great animal but meaner'n the devil, though I guess she can handle him. She's great with horses."

"How nice," Kristen said coolly and the hand on her thigh tightened.

"You're not still jealous of Honey, are you? I thought I explained all that."

She stiffened. "I was never jealous of Honey," she corrected him primly. "And it's certainly none of my affair who you—"

"Relax," he commanded and pulled her back against him, "or I might just start asking questions about the evening you and Roger spent together." His voice was light enough, but she was unsure of the undercurrents. She cast about for a question that would put her on safer ground—she certainly did not want to discuss Roger with Clay.

"How far is it to Goliad?" she asked finally.

"Fine historian you are," he rebuked her. "Don't you recall how far Bonham had to ride from the Alamo when he went trying to get help?"

"You're the guide on this expedition, remember?" she retorted.

"It's all right with me if you want to be shown up at your own game," he warned her. "It's about ninety miles —should take us about two hours more or less. You'll like the Presidio La Bahía. They've been working quite awhile restoring it and it's all finished now. But personally I prefer the Mission Espíritu Santo. It's much prettier."

Kristen looked at him wonderingly. "How is it you know so much about the history around here?" she asked. "When we first met, you didn't seem a bit interested in history."

He shot her a glance. "When we first met, I *wasn't* a bit interested in history—right then. I had other things on my mind entirely. And I still do, for that matter," he added with a grin. "But this is my country around here. I grew up with it."

Ignoring the first part of his statement, Kristen realized how little she knew of him and his family, where and how he had grown up. "Tell me about yourself, Clay," she invited.

But he shook his head. "There's little enough to tell. And all rather commonplace and boring."

Unconsciously she leaned closer to him. "Please tell me, Clay. I'd like very much to know."

He gazed at her for a moment with an inscrutable look

91

and then turned his attention back to the highway; his hand moved slightly along her thigh.

"I grew up a little to the west of here on a small farm. My dad should never have been a farmer, but he didn't know anything else, so he stuck with what he had. It took all his time and effort just pulling a living out of that land of his. It was good land, I discovered later, but Dad just didn't know what to do with it.

"I was working my way through agricultural college when I met Shorty—he was doing the same. After we finished, we decided the thing to do was to try our luck at ranching and put to use all that stuff we'd been studying. So we pooled our assets—which were not much at the time—and with Jake Moore's help we've managed to pull it off." Kristen, watching his face, saw him smile. "We couldn't have done it without Jake; the Moores have been more like family than my own."

"Where's your ranch, yours and Shorty's?"

Clay raised his hand and gestured. "Not too far from here—just south of San Antonio. It's not a large spread, but we've got some fine cattle. I'd like you to see it."

For some reason her breath caught. "I'd like very much to see it, Clay."

There was no more talk and after a while Kristen felt her eyelids growing heavy; last night had contained very little sleep. She tried to stifle a yawn.

Clay moved his head around until his lips rested on her cheek. "Sleepy?" he murmured.

She nodded. "I always get sleepy riding in a car."

Raising his hand, he pressed her head down on his shoulder. "Put your head down there on my shoulder and take a nap. There's not much to see until we get there."

Kristen started to raise her head, but he pressed it back firmly. "But you can't drive this way," she protested.

Clay sighed. "Must you always argue with me?"

In a moment she found herself dozing off and later,

when she began to wake, the first thing she was aware of was a hand moving slowly along her thigh. She awoke fully to find that her head had moved down until it rested on his chest and her right arm was thrown over him and around his waist. Jerking her head up, she saw that he was grinning, his hand still moving.

"Nice," he remarked. "Did you have a nice nap?"

Sitting up stiffly, Kristen set about trying to straighten her hair, ignoring him as best she could and wondering how she could ever have allowed herself, even in sleeping, to get herself into such a position.

"How long did I sleep?"

"We're almost there. I've made good time with just one hand—and it's been quite some time since I've driven this far with only one hand."

Her look was disbelieving. "You do it amazingly well," she retorted, "with so little practice."

The old historical town of Goliad was small but picturesque, but after a short ride through the town Clay announced that he was starving.

"There's a picnic area near the Mission Espíritu Santo, so we'll go there first and I'll make some inroads on those doughnuts. We'll have the picnic lunch later, if that's all right."

Before they reached the river, Kristen could see the tall spire of a mission thrusting itself above the trees and began to point excitedly.

"Is that it? Is that La Bahía?"

Clay shook his head at her ignorance. "Fine historian you are," he chided. "That's Espíritu Santo. The Presidio La Bahía is on the other side of the river. We'll be seeing it later. But first things first—we eat!"

He turned off on a small road leading past a square gray building marked museum, and back from it, up a long sweeping hill of neatly mown grass, was the mission. Seeing it, Kristen caught her breath. Clay had said it was pretty, but in his masculine way he had understated the truth. It was the loveliest thing she had ever seen and the setting was breathtaking. Perched by a crumbling rock wall, the tall, stately edifice had a queenliness about it. It seemed to look down from its heights with a certain beneficent indulgence toward the modern structures around that neither enjoyed its antiquity nor had withstood the test of time.

"Can't we go in now and eat later?" she begged, but Clay's stomach was not to be denied.

"We eat first," he reiterated, "and sight-see after. If I don't get something inside me, I'll fold up on you and you'll have to carry me around."

Kristen fought down her eagerness, and when Clay stopped the car under a tree near a picnic table, she reached down to dig out the coffee thermos and the doughnuts.

"Are you quite sure this is going to be enough?" she inquired sweetly. "There's only a dozen here."

Clay took the thermos and headed for the table. "No sarcasm," he warned. "Just remember, if I hadn't used my strong-arm tactics on you, you might not even be here."

She acknowledged that he was probably right and asked if he might spare her a doughnut.

"Have two," he said generously. "Keep your strength up. You'll probably need it."

She took a bite and chewed it thoughtfully. "And just what's that supposed to mean?" she asked after she had swallowed.

"You've got an evil mind," he accused her. "I just meant that climbing around old ruins can be hard work. What else?"

She gave him a look and resumed her eating, looking back from time to time up the slope to the mission.

When he had finished the last of his coffee and at least a half-dozen doughnuts, Clay announced he was ready to go. They drove the car back up to the museum, parked in the small parking lot, and made their way through the gate and up the walk to the mission. There was a small stone marker stating that this was indeed the Mission Espíritu Santo de Zuñiga; it had been at this location since 1749 and had been founded by Father Antonio Margil de Jesus, a member of the Franciscan Order.

After having read the marker, Kristen started on up the walk to the mission, but Clay reached out and held her back.

"Look over there." He pointed across the river to the southwest. "You can see the Presidio La Bahía." Despite the modern buildings around it and the busy highway, it was still most imposing. "Espíritu Santo's protector," Clay said after a moment, "and I suppose it was a fairly capable one in those days." He took Kristen's arm and turned her back toward the mission. "It looks serene, doesn't it? As if it had all the confidence in the world that it could last another couple of centuries at least, and that La Bahía would see that it did."

The buildings were now in good repair and, walking through the rooms, they were able to reconstruct in their mind's eye how it must have been in times long past. Walking around the outside, they could see, along the main structure, the long outer building that had contained the kitchens, workshops, and the granary; it was here that the friars carried out their duties. The interior of the church was now bare of furnishings and, unlike many of the old mission churches, was not used for services.

Standing in the vast empty nave of the church with its vaulted ceiling, Kristen gazed around at the altar rails, the pulpit rising to her right and fastened to the wall above her head. Turning to look behind her, she gave a squeal of delight on seeing the steps leading up to the choir loft. She mounted these with Clay behind her and was even more surprised to find a room opening off to her left, which

95

contained another old stairway going up to a window at the top. This stairway had been hewn from a single log which was about a foot in width, the steps being formed by V-shaped notches cut at intervals in the log.

"Can I go up?" she asked.

Clay shrugged apprehensively. "It looks solid enough, but I'll stand by to catch you just in case the whole thing should come crashing to the floor."

With these words to encourage her Kristen made her way slowly to the top and leaned forward cautiously upon the thick windowsill in order to peer out the window.

"Clay!" she exclaimed in an awed voice, "I can see for miles."

"And that, sweetheart, was the idea," he said, laughing, but she was too excited to pay him any notice.

"And I can see La Bahía."

Clay looked up and frowned. "You'd better come down from there before you fall off—and come down slowly."

She took a last long look and inched her way back down. "Are you going up?" she asked him breathlessly when she reached the bottom. "The view is simply splendid."

"Not me," he replied with certainty. "I'm a little up on you in weight, and if it didn't hold, I seriously doubt if you could catch me."

Kristen left Espíritu Santo casting a wistful look back over her shoulder. "She's so lovely. And you know," she added after a last brief study, "with all its queenliness, it looks like a she."

Clay laughed, taking her arm and guiding her down the walk. "Then I'm sure La Bahía will look like a he. And I guess that's as it should be, since it was a fort built to protect his lady friend here."

And Clay had been right, Kristen thought, as she walked up to the entrance of the old fort; it did present a sterner countenance than its counterpart across the river.

The restoration, she saw, had been completed to perfection. As they walked into the building, they found the first rooms had been turned into a museum; then came the kitchen, furnished much as it had been in earlier times, and beyond that a wide open quadrangle.

The *presidio* was walled on all four sides with the chapel tucked into the corner. Clay and Kristen walked along behind the walls; the sunshine was rich and warm and a brisk breeze was blowing, whipping the two flags flying overhead until they slapped and popped. One was the red, white, and blue Lone Star flag of Texas; the other, the grimmer flag of Goliad with its bloody arm with the hand clutching a bloody knife.

They walked slowly around the inside of the walls, enjoying the quiet of the afternoon, unhurried until they arrived back at the chapel.

Clay walked over to open the door, saying, "This church is one of those in operation, so to speak. By that I mean they still have services here. But we can go in if you'd like. There's a fresco I think you'd like to see. It's quite imposing."

The chapel was well furnished, some old pieces fitting comfortably with the newer ones; the altar cloth reflecting the flickering of the candles and their light was caught up again in the polished wood of the altar railings. The fresco, which covered the entire wall behind the altar and was, Kristen thought, somewhat overwhelming, was of the Annunciation and pictured an angel with magnificent wings outspread, speaking to Mary, who was seated before him, pondering the enormity of the message she had just received.

"The painting is beautiful, Clay," she whispered, for the quiet of the chapel seemed to call for whispered conversation.

"It isn't old," he whispered back, "at least not when

compared with the rest of this, but it fits in quite well, I think."

Then he added, quite irreverently for such hallowed walls, "Let's go. There's more to see, more notes for you to take, and before long I'm going to be hungrier'n blazes."

Kristen shook her head and turned toward the entrance. "I really pity your wife, provided you ever find one. She'll probably spend all her time in the kitchen."

"Now that you've brought it up," he turned to her, "are you interested?"

She turned to him with a sharp retort forming on her tongue, but it died unspoken. His tone had been light, but it was belied by the smouldering look that had come into his eyes. She was not sure just how she came to be in his arms, but in the next moment he was holding her and his lips were pressing down on hers.

Abstractly she wondered why she always had this queer sinking feeling that moved all through her each time Clay began to kiss her. She had never felt this way when Roger . . . but then Roger would never have kissed her as Clay was doing. Roger's kisses were always tempered with restraint; Clay knew little about restraint. His kisses seemed to have one purpose in mind and that was to carry her past all the limits of her ability to resist him.

It was quiet and still in the chapel, the only sounds being those of the whispered words that Clay spoke into Kristen's ear in the short spaces between kisses. Vaguely she was aware of the flickering light of the candles; the colors of the fresco ran before her half-closed eyes. Her heart was pounding; she could feel the beating of his as he held her close.

It was the murmur of voices and the shuffling of footsteps along the walk outside the entrance that brought her up short. Considerably shaken, she began to push frantically at his chest.

"Clay, please!" she whispered in a tight voice when finally her lips were freed. "Someone's coming!"

He murmured something she was unsure of and released her just as the door swung open and a man with his wife and their three small children walked into the chapel. Kristen was thankful for the shadows that hid her mussed hair and sadly crooked lipstick, and that the parents were too engrossed in their own affairs to give them much notice.

The harassed wife was warning the small ones to keep their hands to themselves—"Don't touch that, Robert!"—while the father, blissfully unaware of the fact that another of his brood was trying to climb into the baptismal font, was reading from a folder.

". . . was painted in 1946 by Antonio Garcia . . ."

Kristen strove to pat her disarranged hair into place while Clay watched with open amusement.

"Do you sometimes get the feeling, my dear"—he leaned to whisper into her ear—"that I'm trying to involve you in an unsavory nook-and-cranny love affair?"

"You wouldn't look so smug, my sweet," she hissed back, "if you could see how crooked your lipstick is."

Surreptitiously, under the guise of giving a closer inspection to the confessional, Clay administered his handkerchief and then led Kristen back out into the small courtyard.

She blinked against the sudden sunlight, while Clay, glancing back inside, got a quick glimpse before the doors swung shut of young Robert making a headlong dash toward the altar with his mother close on his heels.

"If they would give Robert a little time to himself, all the lovely restoration would have to be done all over again. He looks like a very capable chap." Then he added, somewhat ruefully, "I hate to rush you, but it'll be dark before too much longer and—"

Kristen laughed. "I know—you're starved!"

CHAPTER 11

When they reached the park, Clay drove past the tables until he found a remote spot where the grass grew thickly and was secluded in a clump of trees.

"We'll just spread the lunch here instead of on one of the tables. It's a lot cozier."

Kristen glanced around at the empty picnic grounds. "We seem to have it all to ourselves, don't we?" she remarked.

Clay set the box down on the ground and looked around. "Yes, we do seem to be alone, finally. Seems like every time we've been together, there's always been such a crowd of people about." His eyes were watching her closely now. His voice was quiet. "You seem uneasy, Kristen. You're not, by some chance, afraid to be alone with me, are you?"

She did not answer directly but countered by asking another question.

"And should I be?"

"I don't know," he answered truthfully after a moment and began to unload the lunch.

After a moment's hesitation while she pondered his answer, Kristen came to kneel beside him and proceeded to pull the assorted items out and to lay them on the grass.

"I'm not sure what she put in," Clay told her. "I just told her to make sure it was a lot."

The waitress had quite obviously taken him at his word.

There was a whole fried chicken, some sliced ham, cheese, and potato salad in a small ice chest, along with pickles, various relishes, and an apple pie. There was also another thermos of coffee.

Kristen looked at all the food laid out before them and exclaimed: "How many did you tell her were going along on this picnic—a dozen?"

Clay looked at the array with satisfaction. "She's packed lunches for Shorty and me before," he explained, "and I guess when I said for two, she just naturally thought we were together again. Shorty and I can put away a good deal of food," he added as he accepted the filled plate she offered him and fell to with alacrity.

Although she had eaten very little that day, Kristen did not feel especially hungry, but everything smelled and tasted so good she found herself matching Clay in quality of appetite if not in quantity of consumption, for that would have been impossible. She watched in open amazement at the amount he managed to put away, and when he had at last finished and had heaved a long contented sigh and lain back on the grass beside her, declaring he now felt a great deal better, she shook her head in open wonder.

"I can't understand why you're not perfectly miserable," she marveled. "Do you know you've finished off at least half that chicken—not to mention a whopping portion of everything else?"

To this Clay nodded complacently. "You can't seriously expect a guy to go from breakfast to supper on just six paltry doughnuts, now can you? Why that's not only unhealthy, I'm sure it's also downright un-American."

Kristen, sitting next to him, swung around to lean toward him. Looking down at him, she said accusingly, "You mean you had breakfast?"

Clay was suddenly contrite. "That's right, you didn't. All you'd had today was that one doughnut. And me doing all that talking about starving. My word, woman, you must have been about to fall out!"

She laughed and shook her head. "No, it wasn't as bad as all that. I was enjoying myself and I wasn't even thinking about food. Besides, my appetite isn't quite as great as yours, or my needs as pressing."

By the look that flashed across his face she knew that her choice of words had been unfortunate. He lay perfectly still, looking up at her; she remained as she was, leaning slightly forward, propped up on her arm with her hand resting near his head.

The light was fading rapidly now; his face had become a blur and she was unable to read the look in his eyes, but she could feel them watching her through the darkness. Then in a slow, deliberate movement he put his hand up and shifted the arm that she had been leaning upon, turning her so that she was now lying upon her back looking up at him. Above him she could see the darkness of the trees and the sky only faintly lighter, now sprinkled generously with stars. For an instant neither of them moved; around them the night was quiet and still.

Then slowly he lowered himself until his chest was pressing firmly against her breasts; she could feel the hard hammering of his heart against hers. As he began to kiss her, the familiar sinking feeling returned, but now it was accompanied by a surging, burning sensation moving through her body. His hands caressed and the sensations his fingertips brought caused her to tremble. His lips moved from hers; his breath was warm as he spoke.

"You're trembling, sweetheart," he murmured, his lips moving along her cheek, her neck. "Hasn't at least one of the men you've known before me ever made you feel this way?" And when she did not answer, his voice became more insistent. "Tell me."

Her voice sounded strange to her ears, distant, hollow. "No," she faltered, "no one."

Then again his mouth claimed hers and Kristen, under the growing aggressiveness of his lovemaking, felt her control sliding away; her arms, which had been resolutely pressed to her sides, now went slowly up and around his back, pulling him closer to her. She heard him speak, but the words spoken into the hollow of her throat were muffled, unintelligible.

"Clay?" Her question was barely audible.

"I love you, Kristen." His voice was deep, constricted. "I've never told that to a woman before. And you love me. Tell me. Tell me that you love me and that you want me."

Almost imperceptibly he felt her stiffen. His voice softened; his words a caress. "Don't freeze up on me, Kristen. Not now. Just let me love you. Don't be afraid of me, or of yourself. Don't be afraid to be a woman and to love me completely."

Now Kristen was exerting the full extent of her control and was shaken by the violence of her emotions. She wanted with a sudden desperation to tell him what he wanted to hear: that she loved him and yes! that she desired him. But she forced back the words. To say them would destroy all her defenses against him and leave her open.

But now his whispers were causing her to lose control of her thoughts; his kisses and caresses were becoming more intimate. She fought down a growing panic. No man had ever demanded this of her with such overwhelming determination; no man had ever torn aside her barriers, stripped her emotions bare as Clay was doing now.

And yet there was no sense of his forcing himself on her. Truthfully all she could feel from him was the love he had said he had for her. And the warmth, and the caring.

Yet to Kristen somehow this had become more than that. It had become a test between his will and hers. She could not let him control her in this manner, even if his control was his love; she had to withstand the demands he had no right to make on her. Even if he did love her and she loved him, he had no right to do this to her, to reduce her to this state of emotional chaos.

"Clay, stop." She said the words as short and as even as she was able and Clay drew up instantly.

He had felt her grow rigid in his arms; her body, which had been pliable and yielding to his touch, was now stiff and resisting. He did not release her and she spoke again.

"Clay, let me go."

There was a faint note of entreaty and he shook his head. "Kristen," he said softly, "you don't have to worry. I'm not about to do anything against your will." There was something in his voice that caused her to knot up suddenly inside. It was as if she could all at once feel his pain. "You don't have to worry," he repeated, sounding resigned, "you've got the situation well under control."

In one movement he released her, rolled over, and sat up. He sat there for a long moment before he spoke again.

"I wish you could make up your mind just what you want from me."

The frustration was in the evenly spoken words. She heard it and it left her feeling suddenly miserable and cold when she should have felt only relief. She sat up slowly and saw his profile in the light of the moon, which had risen without her knowing it. The silence was unbearable to her, but it took all the courage she could muster to break it.

"Clay, I'm terribly sorry."

When he turned to her, the look on his face caused her heart to twist painfully.

"It's late, Kristen," he said quietly. "I'd better get you home."

She watched him as he began methodically to repack the lunch things in the box. She watched him and knew he was not ignoring her to punish her, pouting like a small child who has not had his way. She knew that he still wanted her and was holding himself in check with difficulty. And she knew she had hurt him, and deeply.

She felt a quick rush of pity and gratitude toward him, but she did not give voice to her feelings. Pity and gratitude were very poor substitutes for the love that he wanted from her.

The ride home was conducted in a heavy silence. Kristen sat in a miserable knot in her corner of the seat, knowing that it was her own actions that had put her there and remembering with longing the warmth of their trip down. She glanced at Clay's face from time to time only to find the closed mask was still in place. She remembered also the many times she had rebuffed him and did not wonder that he had pulled away as he had. How many times does one come back asking to be hurt? she found herself wondering. And his eyes never looked her way but remained staring at the road in front of him.

After they had been on the road for about an hour, Kristen felt her eyelids growing heavy, and despite the existing strain, she fell asleep. When she awoke, she saw they had pulled up in front of the house; she had no idea how long they had been parked there. Clay was sitting quietly, and although his face was hidden in the shadows, she knew he was looking at her.

It was late, she knew, for there was no traffic, no lights on in the houses, and she tried to see the face of her watch by the light of the streetlamp but could not.

"It's nearly one o'clock."

His voice was no longer tight and the reserve so evident before had disappeared, but when he leaned forward slightly and the dim light fell across his face, she could see the grim lines still etched about his mouth.

"I'm not going to apologize, Kristen," he told her, "for anything that happened. You may be able to tell yourself that you don't love me, but you can't lie to me. You have some problem and your mind is all screwed up trying to work it out. Well, your mind may be slow catching on, but the rest of you is responding and I just want you to understand that I'm not through trying to reach you. To touch that wonderful woman you are deep inside. And this other fellow, whatever he's been to you, whatever his prior claim, I'm not stepping aside." His mouth tightened. "Not even a little."

With that he got out of the car and opened the door, but when she stepped out, he stood blocking her way.

"I probably won't see you tomorrow," he explained, "because I've got to go to the Moores' and give them a hand, but I'll probably see you the day after. I'll call."

She had kept her head down, not sure that she wanted to meet his eyes, but with these words it snapped up. Her surprise was evident. His smile twisted.

"Did you honestly think I'd give up so easily?" He placed his hands on her shoulders; his fingers pressed slightly. "I should warn you that I intend to keep right on at you until you admit that you love me and can't live without me. Until you're ready to give yourself to me fully and without restraint—and I don't mean some one-time affair, I mean for the rest of your life."

His fingers gripped tighter as he pulled her to him; his mouth moved close to hers with his lips touching hers as he spoke.

"You want me to come back, don't you?" He felt the tremor pass over her as his arms slid around her, holding her close. "Don't you?"

Mutely she nodded, but his hand came up to grasp her chin and tip her face up to his.

"Say it, Kristen. I want to hear you say it." Kristen moved against him, seeking to turn her head from him, but he held her fast. "Say it, sweetheart, for your sake if not for mine. Admit that you want me to come back. Admit that much."

Frustrated tears filled her eyes and her voice broke

when she tried to speak. "Yes . . . yes, I want you to come back. Now will you let me go?"

But instead of releasing her, he kissed her long and with feeling. "Remember that, and think about all I've said."

He opened his arms and she moved out of them and ran up the steps and onto the porch. When she slipped quietly in through the front door, she glanced back to see that he was still standing there. A moment later she heard him drive away.

Silently she tiptoed up to her room, being very careful not to awaken anyone; she did not think she could face Mrs. Faraday's innocent questions. Nor did she want to see Alicia's knowing eyes. She undressed and crawled into bed quickly and lay in the dark, staring at the ceiling wide-eyed and sleepless for a time, struggling to sort out all that had transpired. It seemed days since she had been awakened from sleep and dragged away to Goliad instead of only hours.

Why, she asked herself over and over, had he come along? Her life had been nothing but a sad muddle from the moment she first laid eyes on him; her life that she had so well organized, so well planned, was now all mixed up.

And he was not about to give up. He had warned her. He had guessed what her feelings had been when she had made him release her there at the picnic grounds at Goliad. She was constantly holding him at arm's length because he demanded more than she was ready to give. But part of her was responding, Clay knew that. Though something was holding back. Something deeper.

If he would only move more slowly, let her set the pace. Was that it? That he refused to let her set the pace, call the moves, as she had done all her previous life? Her mind gripped the thought and then it eluded her into a fog of sleep.

CHAPTER 12

Kristen awoke the next morning with a slight headache and feeling almost as tired as when she had gone to bed, which surprised her not at all. Between her restlessness and thinking of Clay, with an occasional question about Roger, she had spent the night more awake than asleep. And the worst part was that she had solved none of the problems that continued to plague her even with the morning.

Another shipment had come in and Alicia and Mrs. Faraday were busily uncrating, wads of paper and streamers of excelsior flying everywhere. It had come in yesterday, Mrs. Faraday had informed her, and she was positively beside herself to get back to it.

"Some people—my relatives mostly—think I'm touched in my upper works to spend so much time and money—and I'm sure it's the money part that worries them the most," she added candidly, "gathering all these useless—and those are their words—pieces of junk. But at my age I say money is for spending and if I enjoy my collectings, and I can assure you that I do, then it's none of their business and they can do what they will." She smiled and added, "It'd serve them right if I willed all this to them."

She finished with a twinkle and with an air of defiance that told Kristen she had probably told the said relatives this very thing on more than one occasion. But then the defiance disappeared and Mrs. Faraday heaved a long sigh.

"But Alicia is doing such a good job through her connections in Mexico that I'm sadly afraid some of my things will have to be relegated to the attic. No matter how I push and shove things about," she said ruefully, "I'm getting short on space."

She looked at Kristen with an air of expectancy and Kristen, fearing some of the "treasures" might be relegated to her room, searched through her mind quickly for something to say that would sidetrack her employer for the moment.

"Alicia must have very good contacts in Saltillo," she said finally, "to be able to come up with all of this."

"Oh, yes, my dear, very good contacts. I was so very lucky to find her. She has truly been a jewel."

"Just how did you find her, Mrs. Faraday?" Kristen questioned.

"I advertised in papers here in Texas and in some Mexican papers. She was one of several who answered and came well recommended."

Kristen nodded, relieved that her employer had been safely detoured away from the subject of where to store the overflow of her collections. At least for the time being she was safe—and so was the extra space in her bedroom.

They finished their breakfast and as Mrs. Faraday excused herself and rose to leave, Kristen stood up quickly.

"Mrs. Faraday," she began, feeling out her words, "I'd like to apologize for my fantastic behavior of yesterday. It was inexcusable, but I really—"

Mrs. Faraday smiled knowingly. "But you really didn't have much choice, did you, my dear? That is, if what Maria Rosa told me is correct. With Maria Rosa one can never be too sure you're getting the right of things, but to hear her tell it, he practically dressed you and threw you into the car. Mr. Courtney appears to be a very resourceful young man"—she nodded her approval—"and don't apologize. I'm sure you made plenty of notes and you had a wonderful day to go with them. So all's well after all."

After she had left the room, Kristen sat back down to finish her coffee and wondered what Mrs. Faraday would have said if she had known the entire happenings of yesterday. Being the romantic she was, Kristen thought ruefully, she'd probably have said the same thing, only adding that she thought Kristen was most likely a fool.

CHAPTER 13

Clay drove out to Helotes, turned off on the unpaved road leading up to the large rock house and went inside without bothering to knock. He had been going into that house in just that manner for years. It was early and Jake, his wife Lorene, and Honey were still seated around the table in the spacious kitchen, putting the finishing touches to a fair-sized breakfast.

Jake, glancing up as Clay walked in, took one look and grimaced to himself. Obviously something or someone had been rubbing Clay the wrong way and had succeeded in putting him in a foul mood. He was scowling darkly and looked, Jake thought, as if he would welcome someone saying or doing something he didn't like just so he could plow into them.

The first one to incur his wrath was Honey. Seeing Clay but not having her father's insight, she jumped eagerly to her feet, saying excitedly: "Clay! I'm so glad you're here. You didn't really help me with my horse the last time you were here and I could use some help badly. I can't understand why I can't get that horse to—"

"Good grief, Honey!" he snapped, "you should've known better than to buy an animal you couldn't handle! I always thought that you at least knew something about horses. Guess that just proves how wrong I can be."

Honey's eyes widened, but she paid no real attention to his outburst; she had heard it before. "Well, I'm going out to the stables, but please don't bother coming with me. Stay right where you are and have some of Mother's pancakes and coffee. They'll make a human being out of *almost* anything."

With that she walked out the back door and she could be heard humming as she walked toward the stables.

"What's she so happy about?" Clay ground out. "There's no telling how much money she threw away on that wild animal she calls a horse."

Jake grinned and Lorene got up for another plate. Like Honey, they were both too accustomed to Clay's occasional bouts of ill-temper to let it bother them.

"Sit down, boy, and let Lorene get you something to eat," Jake said calmly, chewing slowly on a piece of ham.

Clay sat down at the table and opened his mouth to speak, but Lorene spoke before he could get the words out.

"And don't say you're not hungry because I've never known you not to be able to eat something. And there's no telling what you two are eating over at your place. Men should never be allowed to cook for themselves."

Clay came as close to grinning as his bad humor would allow; it was almost impossible to remain angry with Lorene around. Therefore, he was glad when she said she had to get on with her work and left them alone; he wasn't ready to give up his bad humor just yet.

"Eat up, boy," Jake told him, "and then we'd better go out and see Honey's horse before she gets all fired up too. We don't need two bad tempers loose on us this morning."

Jake watched Clay as he ate, but he did not ask any questions; he knew something was bothering Clay; he didn't get this worked up over just run-of-the-mill problems. No, this one was a big one and he wondered just what it could be. But he knew Clay well enough to know he would tell him in his own good time. He would just have to wait.

After Clay had put away a good portion of the ham and

pancakes, the two men drove the pickup down to the stables.

As they drove along, Jake said, "I've got some fence I need to get busy repairing down by the tank before the hunters start coming in. Would you be interested in lending me a hand?"

Clay said he would welcome some activity and spoke with such a grim inflection that Jake glanced at him quickly. *Yeah,* he thought, *something sure has the boy in a bad way.*

Jake stopped the pickup outside the stables and they went in to find Honey standing on one of the stall gates leaning over, talking to the horse in a coaxing voice but accomplishing little. The horse stood on the opposite side of his stall and eyed her malevolently, his ears laid back menacingly.

Honey looked up as Clay and her father walked into the barn and climbed down from the stall gate.

"I do believe that's the most obstinate animal I've ever come across. Usually I can make some kind of headway when they're stubborn, but he won't even budge an inch, no matter how much I coax him."

Clay walked over to the stall and gave the horse stare for stare and then turned back to Honey.

"That's got to be the meanest looking—Hey! Cut that out!"

Clay wheeled around while the horse, which had just taken a good-sized nip out of Clay's back, retreated with calm dignity to the back of the stall.

Honey stifled a laugh. "You know, I hadn't been able to think of a name for him," she said, grinning broadly, "but I think I'll just name him Clay—you're both so mean-tempered."

Clay glared at her and strode back out to the pickup, muttering something about not wasting any more time on fool horses and their even more fool owners and getting to the fence mending, where they wouldn't just be wasting their time.

As they drove along the narrow road, Jake talked incessantly about the different ranch problems, of the deer hunters who were soon coming, while he watched Clay out of the corner of his eye. Ever since his flare-up in the stable, he no longer had the dark scowl nor did his eyes flash angrily. It was as if he had spent his anger in that one final outburst and now was content to brood silently.

Jake frowned. There was more to this than simple bad temper; something mighty serious was eating at the boy.

When Jake pulled to a stop beside the water tank, he cut the motor but did not move; when Clay started to climb out, he put a restraining hand on his arm.

"Hold on for a minute, Clay," he said. "Now, I don't want to pry and you know you don't have to answer me unless you want to, but do you want to tell me what's eating at you?"

Clay shot him a quick look and saw the quiet eyes looking at him as they had for so many years with the easy friendship Clay had come to rely on so heavily. He took a deep breath.

"You're going to think I'm a blasted fool when I tell you, Jake, but so help me if you laugh—"

"And when have I ever laughed at any of your problems, Clay?" he asked quietly and Clay nodded.

"I've met this girl, Jake." He looked up and Jake nodded.

"Honey said that she met a girl in San Antonio," Jake commented. "Was that her?"

A tightness came around Clay's mouth. "That was her. She was brought up by foster parents, an aunt and uncle, and they did a fine job, only they let her have her own way too much for her own good. She's a great person and we get along well together, as long as I don't get too close." He paused. "And there's someone else in the picture.

114

Seems he's easier going than I am"—he smiled ruefully—"but then, I guess most people are. He was around before I came along. But he's not what really bothers me. What really bothers me is the way she has of holding herself away, aloof, and she's all wound up tight. I guess none of the men she's ever known before has ever made any demands, and when a normal man comes along, she stays busy throwing up defenses."

Jake allowed his mouth to widen into a slow smile. "I'm not so sure that I'd class you in the absolutely normal category, Clay."

Clay's eyebrow rose. "Well, maybe I am a little forceful at times," he acknowledged, "but I'm convinced that's what she needs. She's having a struggle, but it's mostly with herself. Part of her wants me—and I believe wants me badly—and the other part doesn't. Her problem is she thinks too much. I'll have her going my way and then she'll start thinking and wham! everything's blown sky high."

There was a short silence during which Jake took out his pipe and lighted it while Clay lighted a cigarette.

"Correct me if I'm wrong, Clay," he said, "but it doesn't sound like this is just another woman. It sounds as if it's a good deal more serious. Am I right?"

"You're exactly right," Clay told him. "I've never been more serious in my life. I'm not just looking for someone to go to bed with—that's easy enough to find if that's all you want. But this is different. I've never felt like this about a woman in my life. I really love her, Jake, and I'm no youngster and I know what I want."

"And the girl? Underneath all this does she love you? And what about this other fellow?"

"She loves me. I know that," Clay said with conviction and he ignored the last part of Jake's question. "Although she probably doesn't dare to admit it, even to herself. And that's what makes the whole mess so frustrating. Given the opportunity, she can talk herself in and out of anything that doesn't jibe with the way she thinks things ought to be. But she's finding out that I don't give up easily."

His voice held such a note of determination that for a fleeting moment Jake could almost feel sorry for this girl who had chosen to match strength of wills with Clay Courtney.

"Why don't you bring her out here, to the ranch? We'd like to meet her, Lorene and I."

"I'd like to bring her out here, Jake," Clay was saying, "but she's busy with her job. She's doing research for a historian in San Antonio."

Clay paused; his eyes narrowed.

"Mrs. Faraday is a wonderful woman," he continued, "intelligent, understanding, and completely in accordance with my point of view. Between the two of us we just might be able to pull it off."

CHAPTER 14

Kristen worked steadily through the morning, striving to organize her horribly jumbled notes, rewriting them before they got cold and she forgot what they meant, and pushed all other thoughts aside, declaring that Mrs. Faraday deserved at least one honest day's work for her money.

She stopped briefly for a quick sandwich, wondered fleetingly if Clay would call, and returned to her books convinced that he and Honey were probably up to their necks in horseflesh and too wrapped up in what they were doing to give her a thought.

On her way back through the hall she saw a letter addressed to her lying on the hall table, almost lost amid the clutter. It was from Roger. She took the letter to her room before she opened it. The words, although somewhat stiff, were a balm to her troubled mind; there was nothing demanding or peremptory in the thoughtfully written phrases.

"I would have called," the letter went. "I wanted to hear your voice, but I thought the words might come easier if I wrote them. We miss you . . ."

We, Roger? she thought. *Not I?*

". . .and are hopeful you'll be coming home soon, if only for a short visit."

Her eyes skipped over the local news; Aunt Maude filled her in on all of that. She came to the last sentence.

"Hopefully I'll be able to come to San Antonio again

soon. You're constantly in my thoughts. Until then. With my love, Roger."

She put the letter back in its envelope and laid it aside. *With my love.* She thought about this for a long moment. A soft, sweet love Roger offered her. Not a love that left her feeling as she had never felt before. A love filled with strange, new sensations. The love Clay held for her was a love that asked something in return. With Roger there seemed to be no demand whatsoever.

She went to her mirror and stared.

Is that what you want? she asked herself. *It would make so many people happy—Aunt Maude, Uncle Frank, certainly Roger. But what of yourself?*

She stared; she got no answer, although she stood there for a very long time.

When the knock sounded at the door and Maria Rosa put her head into the room to tell her she was wanted on the telephone, it was already growing dark outside. She knew by the look on the woman's face that it was Clay; doubtless she thought him slightly less than sane.

"Were you afraid I'd forgotten you?" he asked as soon as she had answered and Kristen found herself smiling at his good humor. Nothing seemed to put him out of countenance for long. She did not know what Jake and his family had been putting up with all day.

"How would you feel if I told you that I had not thought about you at all?"

"It would devastate me—if I believed it," he told her. "But my colossal ego won't let me. Will you be able to get away tomorrow and we'll take in the local missions?"

Kristen hesitated, wondering what exactly she wanted. "I'm sure I can, but before you start congratulating yourself on my easy acceptance, let me say that I know you would just go over my head if I said no. Mrs. Faraday is besotted with you."

118

"Good for Mrs. Faraday," he said approvingly. "And you could learn from her. I'll pick you up early, but not as early as yesterday, and we'll make a day of it."

There was a brief pause during which Kristen thought she heard the muffled sound of a yawn.

"Man! Am I tired," he said sleepily. "It's been a long day."

Kristen asked what he had been doing all day and heard him groan.

"I spent the day at Helotes. Jake's a little short of help right now, so I gave him a hand mending some fences. There's always something that needs doing on a ranch. And naturally I tried to give Honey a little help with that animal she bought."

"Naturally," Kristen said before she could stop herself and she was sure she heard him chuckle.

"Good night, Kristen," he said. "I'm just too tired to try to convince you. See you in the morning."

"I warn you," Clay told her the next morning as they prepared to drive away, "that I'm not too carried away with the idea of more missions. What I mean is—when you've seen one mission, as the saying goes—but I'm ready to go, I just wanted to prepare you for any possible lack of enthusiasm."

Kristen looked at him questioningly. "If you care so little, Clay, why are you bothering to take me to see them? Why not let me muddle through on my own?"

"Well, to tell the truth, sweetheart, I don't care where we go or what we see, just as long as you're with me. I thought you understood that."

Their meeting that morning, their conversation, had started out on such a light note that the sudden seriousness in his voice caught her off guard and left her without anything to say.

Instead of starting the car, he took her hand and pulled

her toward him; his fingers and thumb tilted her chin so that she was forced to look up at him.

"Are you still angry with me, sweetheart?" His voice was soft, caressing.

She took a breath to steady her voice; her breathing had quickened. "I somehow got the idea it was mostly the other way around," she answered, forcing the words.

His smile was crooked. "I guess maybe you're right," he admitted as he recalled his foul humor of the day before, but then he forgot everything else for his mouth was hovering temptingly close to hers. Their lips were almost touching when she spoke.

"Clay," she warned breathlessly, "Maria Rosa is probably watching us out of the window. I'm not at all sure what she's thinking about us."

Clay grinned. "Well, I've got a fairly good idea what she's thinking," he said as his arms went around her, pulling her close, "so let's not disappoint her."

And he set about smothering her feeble protests.

"All right," he said a long moment later and with obvious reluctance as he put her away from him, "I'd much rather continue that, but if you must have more missions, we might as well get started."

It was remarkable, Kristen thought, or rather *he* was remarkable. He could very easily have made her feel uncomfortable and their relationship would have become stilted. She had imagined that their next meeting, after such a parting, would be strained and perhaps filled with barbed recriminations from Clay, but there had been none of that.

She could not in all truthfulness say that it was as if nothing had happened; the feeling that they were hanging right on the brink of something was all too evident in the undercurrents of his light banter. It lingered, smoldering, at the back of his eyes and it was there in his touch and in his smile. His conversation, although for the most part

120

light and airy, could abruptly change, leaving her open and unprotected.

That he had not given up was plain to see. He would work slowly, persistently chiseling at and wedging into her weaknesses, all of which he knew so well, until her defenses against him had crumbled.

And he would not be satisfied with just the possessing of her physically; it was deeper than that. He wanted all of her, and she pulled back at the thought. No man, in this day and age, should demand so much of a woman.

Her thoughts turned suddenly to Beth. Maybe that was the type of woman Clay needed. One who could give her all easily and without question, holding nothing back. But to put Beth up against Clay would be like tossing a lamb to a wolf!

She smiled at the simile and Clay cocked an inquisitive eyebrow at her.

"Tell me what you're thinking," he asked her. "From the look on your face it seems intriguing."

Kristen frowned. He always saw too much.

"I was thinking of Beth and Brian and how well they're suited to each other. And how happy they are together."

"She loves him very much, I would say from what little I saw of them, and he loves her equally as much. That's about all it takes."

Kristen turned to him, suddenly intense. "Is it, Clay? Is that really all it takes? There's no more to it than that?"

He put out his hand and took hers, pressing it tightly. His eyes sought hers and held them. "If a man loves a woman and she loves him *enough*," he told her quietly and without undue emphasis, "then they find that all the other problems, however large they might have seemed, can be worked out, begin to fade away or take on a new perspective."

Despite his announced disinterest in the missions, Clay

121

neither rushed her through them nor did he seem in any way bored or impatient. He walked along beside her, smiling indulgently from time to time at her enthusiasm and volunteering a random piece of information every now and again.

"For someone who professes to care little for these missions," she accused him on one occasion, "you have a surprising amount of knowledge about them."

"Not so surprising when you remember that I grew up around here," he responded. "Every time you turned around, some teacher was telling you about all of this, and at the least provocation we were all loaded into a bus and herded over the same ground. Some of it was bound to soak in after a while. Just about the time I was becoming fairly adept at giving the teacher the slip," he recalled reminiscently, "and had just about talked a certain girl into hiding out with me behind the ruins, I graduated."

His eyes were sparkling and Kristen gave him a withering look.

"If you'd like me to think you're joking, I hate to disappoint you. The only part I don't believe is that you didn't manage to bring it off."

They started their tour with the Mission San Francisco de la Espada and then after a tour of the Mission San Juan Capistrano he pulled into another parking lot, saying: "Now surely you've seen this one, for no one should come to San Antonio and not see the Mission San Jose."

Stepping through the gateway into the compound, the first thing Kristen saw was the dominating form of the tall gray church rising majestically above the green of the grass and the trees covering the center of the compound. Clay took her arm and guided her along the pathway that took them by the old Indian houses built into the outer walls. In the northwest corner they came to the old granary, adorned with the stone archways that Clay informed her were called flying buttresses, and he waited patiently while she made her notes.

They made their way through the rooms along the northern wall where the Indians had done the carpentry and weaving and then they paused for Clay to explain the workings of the old mill. Kristen listened politely to the long and detailed explanation, which somehow reminded her of Brian, made various notations, and understood next to nothing of what she wrote.

The workings of the mill was too technical and her attention began to wander. Of its own volition her mind stopped listening to Clay's explanation and she looked about distractedly at the green lawn, the trees, the strutting peacocks with their blue-green feathers. It was a wonderful mixture of colors all under the brilliant blue of the sky. The sun was warm, relaxing.

Then she became aware that Clay's discourse on the mill was drawing to a close and she struggled to get her thoughts in hand. With determination she turned to gaze at the church that they were now approaching.

"Is it true," she asked, pointing toward the rose window, "that the man who carved those beautiful designs had an unhappy love affair somewhere back in Spain and swore to live the rest of his life in celibacy, dedicated to his art?"

Clay grinned broadly at this. "The story I heard was that they are still having a tough time just trying to count the number of his descendants that are living here in San Antonio. Now that's the sort of celibacy I can understand and the only kind I'd be interested in."

After they had finished the Mission San Jose, Kristen had lost all interest in seeing any more missions and, pleading aching feet, asked if they could not just skip whatever was left. Clay nodded his agreement and led her to the car.

123

"What about the rest of the day?" Clay asked as he helped her into the car. "Anything else you want to see?"

Kristen shook her head emphatically. "I've got mountains of information here and if I allow it to get cold, I'll never get the straight of it." She looked at him pleadingly. "Seriously, Clay, I really do need to work the rest of the day. I do have a job, you know."

"All right," Clay conceded, "you've convinced me. Today you work. I've got to keep Mrs. Faraday happy, or she'll cut out my visiting privileges."

CHAPTER 15

Although it was Saturday and Mrs. Faraday demanded little on the weekends, Kristen awoke early. Pulling on a pair of blue slacks and a matching sweater, she went downstairs for breakfast, not surprised to find the room empty, for Mrs. Faraday had told her that she and Alicia would be gone early on a trip to the south Texas town of Refugio. Something about a small statue Alicia had found and which, in some way Kristen had not caught, concerned the mission there. They would be gone most of the day.

She worked in the library through the first part of the morning, leaving the door open so she could hear the phone if it rang. Outside the window she could hear Ramon working in the flower gardens. The man had a way with growing things and Kristen was sure a lot of his outside activity stemmed from the fact that Maria Rosa was in the house.

She had been lost in her work and was brought back to reality when the doorbell rang. She put her pen down but did not get up until she heard Maria Rosa's footsteps on the stairs. Walking to the head of the stairway, she waited for Maria Rosa to speak.

"Señor downstairs, Señorita. In the *sala*."

Kristen went down thinking perhaps Roger had gotten away for the weekend, although surely he would have called first. She pulled up short as she stepped into the room. It was neither Roger nor Clay but Rafael who was standing in front of the fireplace.

"Oh!" she said after a pause, striving not to sound disappointed. "It's you, Rafael. Maria Rosa must have made a mistake, or more likely I misunderstood her. I thought she said you wanted to see me. I'm afraid Alicia isn't here right now. Didn't Maria Rosa tell you?"

"*Sí,* she told me and there was no mistake," he said, stepping toward her. "I told Maria Rosa I wanted to speak with you. She told me Alicia had gone, but I was to meet her this morning. She did not tell me she was to leave town, but when she did not come, I came here. When I heard she was not here, I had to speak with you."

He was now only a foot or so away from her and she resisted with an effort the impulse to take a step backward.

"They have gone to Refugio, Rafael," she told him, keeping her voice quiet and calm. "I'm sure they'll be home by dinnertime—surely not much later. You can see Alicia then and she can explain everything to you."

Kristen regretted these last words instantly, for instead of calming him, they seemed to cause him even more agitation.

"She did not leave a message for me?" His eyes narrowed. "And you are sure she went with the señora?"

So that was the cause of all this emotion, Kristen thought with some relief. Just plain old jealousy. Rafael did not care to have Alicia out of his sight.

"Yes, I'm sure she went with Mrs. Faraday, Rafael," Kristen informed him in a quiet, confident tone, trying to reassure him. "But no, she didn't leave any messages, at least not with me. Perhaps she left word with Maria Rosa. If you'll wait a moment, I'll ask her."

She turned toward the door, but Rafael stepped forward and grasped her arm. "I have asked her," he said in a voice tight with anger. "She knows nothing."

126

His face was close to hers now and she could see his eyes were dilated.

"She would not go without leaving a message." His hand gripped her tightly. "She would not!"

He had by now worked himself into such a state that only Kristen heard the doorbell. He continued to mutter accusations at her, as if she were keeping something from him, but her attention was so taken by the opening of the front door and the ensuing muffled conversation coming from the front hall she gave scant heed to the jealousy-ridden man who was still gripping her arm.

Her heart quickened its beat and relief poured over her as she caught a movement at the corner of her eye and Clay stepped into the room.

His glance took in the situation quickly.

"What in blazes is going on around here?" he exploded.

Startled, Rafael released his hold on Kristen's arm and took two steps backward. Clay stepped forward and Kristen, who had never seen him quite this angry before, caught her breath. His eyes, under the drawn brows, were blazing in a golden wrath; his jaw and his hands were clenching simultaneously.

Kristen stepped forward and placed her hand on his arm. "It's all right, Clay," she said in a quiet voice, hoping to calm him. "He's looking for Alicia and she's not here. He's gotten himself all worked up about it, and now he's upset and doesn't know what he's doing."

Clay took a long breath and then she could feel some of the tension leaving his body as he forced himself to relax. But his eyes were still burning, although his voice was quiet.

"All right, Rafael, Kristen has told you that Alicia isn't here, so that's that. When she comes back, you two can work out your problems between you. So why don't you just go along until she gets back?"

Rafael stood irresolute for a moment, then he cast one

last fleeting glance toward Kristen and, skirting Clay widely, left through the door and was gone. A moment later the front door opened and then closed with a resounding bang.

With the closing of the door Kristen sighed and looked relieved, glad that Clay had come and more than glad that her confrontation with Rafael was over.

Clay stepped to her side and slid his arm around her waist, looking down at her. "Are you okay? I never can make heads or tails out of what Maria Rosa is saying when things are running normally, and when she gets excited, then it's impossible. And when I came in and saw him with you by the arm, I'm afraid I overreacted. What was going on anyway?"

Kristen smiled up at him, feeling a little silly now that it was all over. "I'm all right, Clay. He only upset me because I hadn't expected him to act as he did. He didn't seem to believe what I told him about Alicia. I hadn't known it, but Rafael is a very jealous person."

She sighed and leaned against him. Clay leaned back and tipped her face up so that he could look at her and felt a sudden constriction in his chest. Her hair was tousled about her face and her eyes were wide and brilliantly blue, her lips soft and slightly parted. His arm tightened around her, pulling her close, and he put his hand up, pressing her cheek against his chest. His heart was pounding loudly in her ear, and when he spoke, his voice was unsteady.

"Kristen—"

The front door opened and Kristen stiffened. Clay, still holding her, turned as Ramon stepped quickly into the room.

"Señorita?" he asked, looking toward Kristen with a worried frown. "Is everything all right? Maria Rosa said you were having troubles with Rafael."

Kristen shook her head, smiling ruefully.

"Everything's fine, Ramon. Nothing at all to worry about. Everyone just got a little overexcited, but now everything's under control. But thank you for your concern."

Ramon nodded, continued to frown, and left the room.

Clay turned back to Kristen. "Where is Alicia, by the way? Or Mrs. Faraday?"

Kristen explained that the two women were gone for the day and noticed that Clay frowned. He put her from him gently and sat her down on the couch.

"I've got to make a phone call," he told her, still frowning thoughtfully. "Just hang on a minute."

With that he strode out of the room and disappeared down the hall. After a moment she could hear him talking into the receiver, but she could not distinguish any of the words he was saying.

Sitting and listening to the deep rumblings of his voice, she realized now he had been dressed differently than usual this morning. He had been in tight-fitting jeans and a long-sleeve shirt thrown open at the collar, the sort of clothes he would wear at the ranch.

When he had finished talking and was walking back down the hall, she could hear the heavy footsteps of boots.

When he stepped back into the room, she was amazed at the difference in him; he appeared taller, somehow, and broader and more masculine, if that were possible, than before. His actions were freer, more relaxed in the sort of clothing he was more accustomed to wearing. And there seemed about him an even greater air of confidence and strength.

He came now to tower over her where she sat on the couch; he was still frowning.

"You sure you're all right, Kristen?" His eyes examined her closely. "You're looking sort of strange to me."

She smiled, nodded, and with a gesture indicated his different type of clothing. "It's you who are different," she told him. "I've never seen you dressed like this before. It changes you, in a way."

A look came into his eyes she could not read. "Better get used to it," he advised, "because this is usually it."

"Oh, I'm not complaining," she said hastily. "It's just you look larger than life somehow." Then a thought struck her. "You're going out to the Moores', aren't you?"

She had struggled to sound matter-of-fact about it, as if it didn't matter—she didn't want him to accuse her of being jealous of Honey again. If she failed, he did not show that he had noticed.

"I was going back home," he told her simply, "and I was coming to tell you good-bye."

Her eyes widened and she was totally unprepared for the feeling of dismay that swamped her.

He came and sat down beside her. "I said I *was* going home, but I've decided to stay on for another day. I can't go off and leave you here alone with Rafael having a jealous fit and taking it out on you. I'm sure everything will be all right when Mrs. Faraday is here and Alicia comes back to straighten him out. She can probably handle him right enough, but until then I'll just stick around to see that all goes well."

Kristen was torn between being happy that he was staying and not liking the fact that she was responsible for his feeling he should stay.

"Why did you decide to leave?" she asked.

"I didn't—the mares did. Shorty called me last night and told me I needed to get that stud down there, and there are other things that need doing." His smile twisted. "I've been away a lot longer than usual."

She felt another pang of conscience. He was needed at the ranch and she had kept him here, was still keeping him here. She took a deep breath.

"You don't have to stay here on my account, Clay. I doubt if Rafael will come back. And once he gets over this

130

bout of jealousy, he'll be all right. I've never had any trouble with him before and anyway it's not me he's angry with, I just happened to be the only one here. I'm quite sure I'll be—"

"You'll be fine," Clay interrupted her, "because I'm taking you out of here for the day. A just-for-fun day with no history, no notebooks, no worrying about your job. We'll spend the day at the zoo," he told her with a grin.

"At the zoo!" She was incredulous. "But the mares . . . the stud . . ."

Clay laughed. "All that can wait until tomorrow," he assured her. "That was Jake I called," he went on, ignoring her argument, "and I told him I'd be by in the morning and to call Shorty and tell him not to expect me until then, so it's all set." He got to his feet, pulling her up beside him. "Are you ready?"

Hesitantly she nodded, putting her hand to her hair.

"Believe me, it looks fine," he told her and then glanced down with a raised eyebrow at his faded jeans, the unpolished boots. "But I'm afraid I'm another story—I hadn't intended to go anywhere but here and the ranch."

She surprised him by slipping her hand into his and pressing it firmly. "You look great. And every female we meet will be envious of me." And she looked up at him and smiled. "Why are you looking at me that way?" she asked.

"You'd better take it easy, sweetheart," he warned, smiling back down at her. "I react strongly to that sort of behavior—it does terrible things to my control."

She lowered her lashes slowly; her pulse had begun to race oddly. "I think I'll just take my chances," she said and raised her eyes to meet his squarely.

Clay turned west off Broadway into the vast area known as Brackenridge Park and drove for a while down the winding roads through dense and unmolested woods and undergrowth. The tall oaks were now clothed in the rich browns and russets of autumn, while the vines and bushes beneath, protected from the cooler air, remained bright and green. The river rippled quietly through the tangle, twisting and turning, its smooth waters churned now and then by the leisurely paddleboats.

They passed riders on horseback making their way down the narrow bridle paths, but Clay dismissed this sport with a contemptuous wave of the hand.

"It's all right for some people, I suppose," he conceded, "but I'd rather do my riding on the open range. It's much too cramped up trying to ride like this. You've got to have room. I've got a great horse myself—gentle as a baby but spicy as a woman and just about the best cutting horse in these parts." He grinned. "At least that's my opinion." He turned to Kristen as if a thought had just struck him. "You do ride, don't you?"

She cast him a wary look. "Rather indifferently, I'm afraid," she admitted with some hesitation, feeling in some way that she was letting him down.

He turned to look at her. "You're not scared of horses, are you?" he asked as if he were afraid she might say yes.

Kristen shrugged. "I wouldn't say scared, exactly," she equivocated, "just unacquainted with them. You see, the only chance I've ever had to ride has been on paths just like these," she added apologetically.

Clay relaxed as if he were relieved. "Oh, well, once you've grown accustomed to riding, you'll love it," he assured her and she remained tactfully silent.

They spent a few moments walking through the Sunken Gardens, an oriental affair complete with pagoda-style buildings, arched bridges, brilliant flowers, banana trees, and dark pools filled with lily pads and the glittering flashes of huge, fat goldfish. They ate a sandwich in the small restaurant and then made their way to the zoo.

It was late when they arrived back at the Faraday house. And only after checking to be sure Mrs. Faraday's car was back in the garage did Clay walk Kristen up to the porch, where he declined her invitation to come in.

"Sorry, but I've got an early day tomorrow."

He placed his hands on her shoulders and stood looking down at her for a long moment. He began talking to her, but she was not really listening, for her mind was filled with the thought that he was leaving, and despite all his talk about not forgetting her, she would probably never see him again.

And would it matter so much to her if she did not?

She gave herself a mental shaking—she would not allow it to matter that much; and taking a firm hold upon herself, she looked up at him.

"I want to thank you, Clay," she began with controlled politeness, "for taking so much time off to help me with my work. You've really simplified matters for me and I do appreciate all that you've done."

He let her ramble on without interruption until she had had her say. "Have you finished?" he asked when she stopped talking.

"Well, yes, I guess I have," she replied uncertainly.

"All right, now it's my turn. First off, to blazes with your work and with your appreciation," he stated with his usual bluntness. "As I have told you before, I did all this for only one reason and that was to be with you. And don't think you're done with me, because you're not."

His hands slipped from her shoulders and his arms went around her, pulling her to him. His lips touched hers, brushing lightly across them before pressing down firmly. And despite all her intentions that she was going to remain calm and unemotional about his leaving, she felt the well-known sinking feeling returning. But now it was accompanied by a newer feeling, an aching that she knew was resulting from the knowledge that he was leaving, that tomorrow he would not be calling or coming to pick her up, she would not be seeing him smile, or hearing him laughing.

"Think of me," he told her, his lips at her ear, and then he was gone.

CHAPTER 16

Clay pulled the horse trailer past the house and stopped near the stables, pressed his hand on the horn, and then crawled out, yelling: "Manuel! Lorenzo! Get out here and help me get this—"

"You can quit the hollering anytime now, Clay," a quiet voice cut in. "They've gone back to sunny Mexico."

Clay wheeled around to see Shorty coming down from the lower end of the stables. He had a two day's growth of beard and his eyes were red-rimmed from lack of sleep.

"You look like the very devil," Clay informed him.

Shorty scratched at his beard. "Well, that's good," he said amiably, " 'cause that's exactly what I feel like."

Clay frowned. "What's this about Manuel and Lorenzo?"

Shorty took out a crumpled pack of cigarettes, but finding it empty, he jammed it back into his pocket. "Got a cigarette?" he asked and Clay handed him a pack, waited for him to light up, and watched as he automatically pocketed the borrowed cigarettes before he asked his question again.

"Well, where are they?"

Shorty exhaled on a long breath. "Like I said, they've gone back to Mexico. I'm not exactly sure what happened, but there was some family crisis and they felt they had to get down there and help out. Anyway, they've gone and things are in one grand mess around here." He glanced

135

toward the horse trailer. "Got the stud?" Clay nodded. "Well, that's one good thing," he commented and then turned toward the corral behind him. "I'll get the gate and you back up the pickup."

The two men unloaded the horse from the trailer in silence and then headed for the house for a quick lunch before getting back to work. Shorty put some bacon into a frying pan while Clay got out the coffeepot.

"Well?" Shorty said when the bacon was frying and the coffee perking.

Clay glanced around and then resumed cracking eggs into a bowl.

"Well what?"

"Oh, man, don't you 'Well what?' me! I'm the one who had to sit around here for days listening to you carry on and complain about wishing you'd never set eyes on that female, until you finally took out of here after her, remember? Then you come dragging back in here with that closed look on your face and say 'Well what?' Let's have it, buddy. Did you find her, and if you did, was she worth the trip?"

Clay picked up a fork and started beating the eggs. "Oh, I found her quick enough."

Shorty's eyebrows flew up. "Quick, my foot! You've been gone a blasted week!"

Clay laughed. "I missed you too," he said as he stirred the eggs into the pan. "Oh, by the way, Honey sends her love."

"She did, huh?" Shorty set the bacon on the table and poured the coffee while Clay scraped the eggs out of the pan. "Well, I hope you kept your eyes off Honey and concentrated all your efforts on what's her name."

There was a brief pause while Clay spooned sugar into his coffee and stirred it slowly.

"I intend to marry her, Shorty," he informed his friend quietly.

"You what?"

Clay swallowed a mouthful of eggs before he spoke again. "You heard me. I said I want to marry her."

Shorty laid down his fork slowly and sat for a time just staring.

"When?" he asked finally.

"As soon as I can convince her that I'm the one she wants, and not this other fellow."

Shorty frowned and shook his head. "This is too deep for me," he declared, picking up his fork again. "Have you asked her?"

Clay shrugged. "Not in so many words, but she knows."

Shorty swore under his breath. "And you're wondering why she didn't just fall into your arms? Or did she? Women are always falling all over you, for some reason I can't understand. Must be some hidden charm—I sure haven't seen it."

Clay grinned. "Before you ramble too far off the subject, I'll tell you that she didn't exactly fall into my arms, but that's where she ended up. It just took awhile."

Shorty contemplated his friend while he chewed and then swallowed.

"From the sound of things I don't think I need to have my suit cleaned anytime soon."

Clay and Shorty had very little time for talking during the days that followed. With both Manuel and Lorenzo gone there seemed to be more work left over at the end of the day than there had been when it started. Clay had planned to return to San Antonio at the first opportunity, but the way the work kept piling up that seemed like never and his humor suffered for it. He began to flare up at the least provocation—or without any provocation whatsoever.

One day in particular he had snapped at Shorty every

time the unfortunate man had ventured to open his mouth until toward evening, pushed beyond the limits of his endurance, Shorty slammed down the saddle he happened to be holding at the time and exploded.

"Man, if you want that woman so bad, I wish you'd get after her! And leave me be! You're worse than some horse with a burr under its tail!"

Clay's eyes snapped angrily and his hands clenched. "Sounds like a good idea to me! I just might do it!" he thundered and then turned and stalked out of the barn.

Shorty stood for a time thinking and staring at the saddle at his feet. He regretted his outburst because he realized the frustration Clay was feeling. Clay was a man of action and decision and this waiting period, which seemed to be loaded with indecision, was hard on him. Shorty sighed. He had known Clay for a good many years now and he had never acted this way about a woman before. He really had it bad.

He put up the saddle and walked through the darkness into the house to find Clay pacing restlessly. Clay glanced up as Shorty came into the room and there was a look of contrition on his face.

"Shorty, I—" he began but Shorty waved it aside.

"Forget it. I have."

Clay looked relieved but resumed his pacing.

"Why don't you call her?"

Clay glanced at his watch and shook his head. "It's too late, and besides I never was any good on the phone—not enough physical contact, I guess." He grinned and took a deep breath. "I've been acting like a fool and we're both dead on our feet. Let's go to bed."

Shorty grinned. "Now that's the best proposition I've had all day."

CHAPTER 17

"Think about me" he had said and that was just what Kristen resolved not to do. Clay had come into her life, made havoc of it, and now he was gone and she was determined not to let it bother her. She set about her work with renewed vigor, and if her absorption in her work was forced now, she was sure with time she would regain her old enthusiasm. Time had been known to do wonderful things and without Clay around to daily cut the ground out from under her she could surely get herself and her emotions back on their usual even keel once again.

Mrs. Faraday had been sorry to know that Clay had gone but had taken it philosophically.

"He'll be back as soon as he can, dear," she had told Kristen soothingly, thinking Kristen was heartbroken over his leaving, an impression Kristen did not bother to correct, knowing the older woman would never have believed her.

What really rankled were the petty, barbed remarks interpolated from time to time by Alicia.

"So Clay has gone back to the ranch. Did he say when he would be back? No? Ah, well . . ."

Her implications were all the more maddening because they were unanswerable. If Kristen had told Alicia she did not care if Clay came back or not, she would have encountered the lifted eyebrow and the knowing look for her pains.

The days seemed to drag by, although she was busier than she had been previously and her work had become more interesting. Mrs. Faraday had now settled down to writing, and taking down her notes and typing them, while more difficult than research, occupied Kristen's thoughts more thoroughly.

Every now and again Mrs. Faraday would interrupt her dictating to ask if Kristen had heard from Clay, and when Kristen was forced to answer that she had not, Mrs. Faraday would tell her not to be upset, men were such poor hands at writing letters. Kristen forbore saying she heard regularly from Roger, or pointing out that even if Clay could not write, at least he could phone. That would sound as if she wanted him to call, and she definitely did not want that.

It was just as well this way, she told herself. He was not going to write; he was not going to phone. And that was just fine because they had not been getting anywhere anyway. Now he was back with Shorty and his gentle but spicy cutting horse, where he could run things to suit him, and she was . . .

Just where *was* she? Her job was interesting enough, but it would soon be over and she realized she was looking forward to her last year of college with a vague sort of dissatisfaction. Once that had been her natural course; now she was none too sure.

Kristen awoke suddenly without being sure what it had been that had awakened her. She had gone to bed late and sleep had been long in coming. Now she lay quite still, almost afraid to move, listening intently. But there were no more sounds, no noises of anyone moving down the hall, only the stillness of the night and the quiet ticking of the clock.

She was reaching out to turn on the lamp when she heard it. It was a groan—a low moan of someone in pain.

140

Switching on the light, she sat blinking at the sudden brightness and then swung her legs to the floor, reaching for her robe. Then she hesitated, drawing her robe about her slowly and wondering what she should do, still slightly muddled with sleep.

Then it came again, but this time Kristen recognized the sound and where it came from. It was Alicia and she was in pain, screaming louder now. With no more hesitation she ran out into the hall and almost collided with Mrs. Faraday. The older woman was dressed in a robe of almost violent colors, loose and flowing—another of her acquisitions, no doubt, probably from somewhere in Mexico. Her gray hair, usually so neat and prim, was flying in all directions.

Without a word the two women turned toward Alicia's door, opened it, and rushed in. Alicia was lying in the bed, twisting and moaning loudly, her knees drawn up to her chest. Mrs. Faraday flipped on the light switch while Kristen ran to the bedside, placing her hand on Alicia's forehead. She turned to Mrs. Faraday, who was leaning over her anxiously.

"She's got a fever," she said quickly and then turned back to the girl on the bed. "Alicia," she said loudly, for the girl did not seem to know they were there, "Alicia, listen to me! What is it? Where is the pain? Do you hear me?"

The eyelids flickered open; she passed her tongue over her lips before she spoke. "Here," she gasped, placing her palm to her side. "The pain . . . I feel sick . . . the pain!"

Kristen looked back to Mrs. Faraday and the older woman nodded.

"Sounds like appendicitis," she announced firmly. "I'll go and call for an ambulance. She'll have to get right to the hospital and quickly. No telling just how long she's been lying in here in pain and not calling out."

Mrs. Faraday padded out into the hall and Kristen

could hear her talking to the operator. "It's all right, Alicia," she said soothingly. "Everything's going to be fine now. We'll have you to the hospital in no time at all. Try to relax. Mrs. Faraday is calling the ambulance now."

Alicia's eyes widened suddenly. "Hospital? I cannot go to the hospital! The crates . . . they are due in today . . . I must help unpack."

Kristen shook her head. This was carrying your work just a bit to extremes. "Don't worry about the crates. I'll see to them."

"Rafael," she murmured. "Call him. His number . . . there in the drawer."

She pointed to the bedside table and indicated almost frantically for Kristen to open it. To calm her Kristen pulled out the drawer and took out a small address book.

"You will call him?"

Kristen could not imagine anything she wanted to do less, but she nodded and was relieved to see Alicia relax slightly. She slipped the book into the pocket of her robe and glanced at the clock. It was almost six in the morning.

By the time the ambulance had arrived, Mrs. Faraday had doffed the brilliant robe and slipped into a simple dress; her hair was stuffed into a hairnet.

"I'll go with her, Kristen, and you can follow later in the car."

Kristen nodded and stood aside as they lifted Alicia and carried her down the stairs and out into the ambulance. Closing the front door, she turned to meet a puzzled and frightened Maria Rosa standing in the hallway.

"It's all right," said Kristen for what seemed the hundredth time. "Alicia has had an attack of appendicitis." She wondered if Maria Rosa knew what the word meant, but she did not have any idea how to say it in Spanish and was too tired to go through any sign-language explanations.

"Why don't you make some coffee while I get dressed," she suggested.

She was relieved when the woman nodded silently and shuffled off toward the kitchen. She wondered distractedly where Ramon was and decided, like most men, he was never around when you needed him.

As she pulled off her robe, she felt the weight in her pocket and remembered the address book; she took it out and tossed it on the table. She dressed slowly and went down for breakfast, not hurrying because she had decided to pick up the crates before going to the hospital. There was nothing really she could do there, and if she had the crates secure, it would serve to satisfy Alicia.

But before leaving she remembered Rafael and went back to her room, picked up the address book, and put it in her purse. She would call Rafael from the hospital when she had learned exactly how Alicia was doing.

Later, with the crates safely in the trunk of her car, Kristen drove to the hospital. She found Mrs. Faraday standing in the waiting room calmly talking to one of the nurses. Seeing Kristen, she motioned to her as the nurse walked away.

"Alicia is fine, my dear. The nurse just informed me that they have taken her into the recovery room and that she'll be there for a little while. They've assured me all went well and that it hadn't ruptured, although it was a near thing."

Kristen, looking resigned, said, "Well, I guess I'd better call Rafael and let him know. I'll find a telephone and be right back."

Going into the booth in the lobby, she thumbed through the address book, filled mostly with names and numbers in Saltillo, Mexico. Finally she found Rafael's number and dialed it. It rang several times before he answered and his voice was thick with sleep.

"Rafael, this is Kristen Ames," she said slowly and

paused a moment for him to digest this. "Alicia has just had surgery for appendicitis. She's all right now and is in the recovery room."

He was fully awake now; his voice clear and sharp.

"Alicia. She is all right?"

"Yes, and if you want to see her, she'll probably be awake later today. Good-bye, Rafael."

And she hung up the receiver. So now that was taken care of, she thought with satisfaction and then realized she had not told him in which hospital Alicia was located. Oh, well, he could call around; she was too tired to call him back.

She returned to the waiting room to find Mrs. Faraday sitting placidly in a chair, and when Kristen suggested she take her car and go back to the house, the older woman shook her head.

"You go along, Kristen. You've not been looking too well yourself lately. There's really nothing to keep both of us here. I'll just stay long enough to see Alicia safely tucked into her bed and then I'll come along. I've made arrangements for a nurse to stay with her, so you see all is taken care of. Were you able to reach her young man?"

Kristen told her that she had. "He'll probably be around soon enough and he can take some of the responsibility off your hands."

She glanced at her watch. Then she looked a little closer. Could it only be ten thirty? She was so tired and yet Mrs. Faraday looked rested and serene. But then, Mrs. Faraday probably slept at night, she thought with a sigh.

She got into the elevator and rode down to the lobby, and when the doors slid open, she found herself standing face to face with Clay.

144

CHAPTER 18

There was a long moment while Kristen was vaguely aware of the elevator doors sliding shut behind her, of people moving about her. And then Clay spoke.

"Thank God you're all right," he said and his voice was a trifle unsteady. "I went by the house and Maria Rosa managed to get some jumble across about an ambulance and that you'd gone to the hospital. All I could think of was that something had happened to you."

He had taken her hands into his and was gripping them tightly, unconcerned that people going in and out of the elevator were watching them curiously. Kristen was also unaware of anyone else except the man standing before her holding her hands. He was back.

Her lips tightened. Yes, he had left, stayed away without a word, and then returned fully expecting her to fall into his arms with rejoicing. With a quick, unexpected movement she jerked her hands free of his grasp; her voice was cold.

"Alicia had an attack of appendicitis, but she's doing very well, and as you can see, I'm fine. I can't understand why you should be so concerned."

Clay did not speak but eyed her with an eyebrow raised. Then after a pause he said, "Come on," and took a firm grip on her arm. "We can't talk here."

She pulled back. "There's nothing for us to talk about, Clay. I don't want—"

145

"But I do," he snapped, "so come on."

She walked along beside him through the crowded lobby fully aware that he was capable of making a scene if she did not. He only spoke once and that was to ask if her car was in the parking lot. And when she told him it was, pointing, he propelled her toward it and waited until she took out the key. Taking it from her, he unlocked the door and then stood aside while she slid onto the seat and then got in beside her.

"Now tell me what this is all about." His voice had lost some of its edge; he was now in firm control of himself, but not a little apprehensive.

Kristen held to her resolve. He was not going to sway her from her decision that she could get along quite well without him, nor was he going to bully her into some sort of submission. She was her own master; she would do as she pleased without him constantly dominating her life.

"It's all very simple, Clay," she began. "After you left, I thought it all over coolly and calmly. I enjoyed being with you while you were here, but after you were gone, I decided we are just not suited to each other. Surely you must see that?"

Clay sat very still; his eyes never left her face. He had come to the hospital filled with anxiety. Often when someone has been terribly anxious and that anxiety is lifted, relief turns to anger. And Clay, Kristen observed, was becoming very angry.

"So you thought it over coolly and calmly, did you?" he said in a tight voice. "Yes, I can just imagine how cool and calm you were. I hate to admit it, but I guess I made a big mistake about you. You see, I was so sure that somewhere under all that cool and calm exterior there was a really warm and alive person, someone who could, on occasion, feel with her heart and not always rely on her mind to guide her. But I can see now I was wrong." He paused. His anger was draining away now and being replaced by a resigned despair. It was a new feeling for him and he did not like it. He continued, seeking to keep his voice even.

"I also had the idea I couldn't get along without you, but I guess I'll have to try. You're too cold, hardheaded, and unbending to know just what you do want." He opened the door and then turned back. "And I hope that Roger has a lot of fortitude because he's certainly going to need it."

She sat very still and watched him as he strode away, his tall figure disappearing amid the parked cars, and wondered what she had done. She felt an almost overpowering weakness; her hand was shaking as she tried to fit the key into the ignition. She drove home and wondered how she had managed, for she had paid small heed to the traffic moving around her. She tried to answer Maria Rosa's questions, said she did not want lunch, and that Mrs. Faraday would not be home for a while.

She was thinking about asking Ramon to remove the crates from her car when her eyes fell upon an envelope lying on the hall table. It was from Aunt Maude. Picking it up, she tore it open automatically as she walked up the stairs. There was nothing of any importance in the letter, just the everyday, homey news that was Aunt Maude: Uncle Frank had been painting the house now that it was cool; she had finished her canning; Roger had come to dinner a few nights back and had asked when she was coming home; the cat had had another litter of kittens.

. . .

Suddenly Kristen was overwhelmingly homesick. She wanted Aunt Maude to exclaim over how tired she looked and how she should eat more for she looked as if she had lost weight; for Uncle Frank to scold her in his soft, apologetic way; for Roger . . .

And what did she want from Roger?

She thought about his quiet, unassuming ways, his con-

147

stant deference to her wishes, and the comfort of his not constantly making her feel unsure as to what she really wanted.

She looked around her room in the Faraday house and felt suddenly terribly alone.

The telephone rang loudly in the quiet house. She walked out to the stairway and looked over the railing into the hallway below, where Maria Rosa was talking into the receiver. Her first thought, to her dismay, had been that it was Clay.

But it was not Clay. It was Rafael. And he wanted to talk to her.

"Tell him I can't talk now. Tell him . . . tell him I'm going out of town for a few days."

Now that she had put the thought into speech, she could not wait to get away. She knew it was not quite fair to Mrs. Faraday to leave her at a time like this, but she would understand, or at least she would not question.

Kristen wrote a hurried note to her employer telling her where she was going and that she would be back by the time Alicia was out of the hospital and to forgive her for deserting her at such a time as this. Then she set about throwing her clothes into her suitcases and within a few minutes, suitcases piled in the back seat, she was headed toward Marshalton.

It was late when she pulled the car into the driveway of the Ames house. Home. And she was so tired and completely empty inside. Aunt Maude would doubtless say it was from having skipped too many meals, but was that really what was causing it? She thought not.

"Good grief, child!" her aunt had exclaimed when Kristen walked into the house. "Don't you look tired. Have you been ill?"

Her greeting from her uncle had been likewise true to form.

"Kris, why didn't you let us know you were coming? You shouldn't have driven on the highway alone at night. That could be dangerous."

Aunt Maude clucked about her, demanding she sit right down and eat and then right to bed; Uncle Frank brought in the suitcases and wanted to know what in the world she had in those crates in the trunk—he couldn't budge them.

Kristen moaned. It was the first time she had thought about the plaguey crates since she had started to tell Ramon to take them out of the car.

"Never mind them, Uncle Frank. They belong to Mrs. Faraday. I'll have to call her the first thing in the morning and let her know where they are." She resumed her eating of a huge sandwich. "How are things at the store, Uncle Frank?"

"Oh, everything's right as rain. That Roger's got a lot of new ideas—really showing people around here what he knows."

Kristen sighed. It was too soon yet to start thinking of Roger. Maybe later she would call him and tell him she was here, but not when she was so tired.

"Beth's coming home tomorrow for a few days," Maude said in her usual matter-of-fact way, pouring a tall glass of milk and setting it purposefully in front of Kristen. "She called us just this afternoon. It's good you've come now so you girls can have some time together."

Kristen heard this with a feeling of happiness mixed with dismay. Beth had X-ray vision when it came to her sister and Kristen did not want to talk about Clay, or Roger. Not now, not yet.

After a rather late breakfast the next morning Kristen put a call through to Mrs. Faraday. She apologized again for having run out on her as she had and for taking the crates, but Mrs. Faraday took everything with her usual aplomb.

"Tut, my dear," she answered, "don't worry about anything and just enjoy your visit. Alicia is well taken care of and as far as the crates are concerned, I wouldn't be opening them until Alicia was back anyway. She does take all this very seriously, I'm afraid. Oh, yes," she added, "did you see Mr. Courtney before you left, dear? Maria Rosa said he came by yesterday morning while we were at the hospital."

"Yes, Mrs. Faraday," Kristen told her slowly, "I saw him. I met him as I was coming out of the hospital."

There was a short pause.

"Is everything all right, Kristen?" she inquired uneasily. "I'm afraid you sound a bit strained."

"No, everything's fine. And I'll be seeing you in a few days."

She sat staring at the phone long after Mrs. Faraday had hung up. So he had not gone back to the house, or phoned her, but then that did not surprise her. Why should he? Hadn't she told him that she wanted nothing more from him?

"Have you finished your call, Kristen?" Aunt Maude asked as she stepped into the hall from the kitchen. "Beth's plane will be in shortly and I wondered if you would mind going out to the airport without me? I've got lunch in the making and your uncle is still down at the store. He spends nearly as much time there now as he did before he turned it over to Roger."

The airport just outside Marshalton was small and Kristen was the only person waiting near the runway when the plane landed and Beth was the only passenger getting off the plane. She disembarked as she did everything else, breezily, talking to the stewardess, her laughter ringing out loudly. Her pleasure at the unexpected meeting with her sister was evident to all those around.

"Kris! How marvelous to see you!" she yelled as she skipped down the steps. "Aunt Maude didn't tell me you were here when I called."

150

The two sisters embraced heartily and Kristen picked up her sister's suitcase. "I wasn't—here when you called, I mean. I arrived last night. Rather unexpectedly."

Beth's eyes rounded. "You didn't get sacked, did you?"

Kristen laughed. "No, I didn't get sacked, and wherever did you pick up that word? Not from Brian, surely."

Beth grinned, unabashed. "From the students," she explained succinctly. "That's one of the few words I hear them say that I dare repeat—even to my sister. Youngsters are certainly outspoken these days."

"Tell me all about it, Grandma," Kristen retorted dryly as she put the suitcase in and slid under the wheel.

She turned the car around and in a few minutes was speeding down the highway back toward town. Beth, who rarely allowed a minute to go by in silence, was strangely mute, causing Kristen to glance at her suspiciously.

"All right, out with it," Kristen ordered. "You look as if you're going to burst any second now. What are you holding back? You know you're no good at keeping secrets."

Beth swung around in the seat and faced Kristen with an eager smile and Kristen was struck by the radiance in her face. Her eyes were sparkling and her face was beautifully flushed. Kristen wondered suddenly if preoccupied Brian realized just how lovely his wife was. But then she recalled what Clay had said—they love each other. Yes, she was sure that Brian realized.

"Tell me, Beth," Kristen urged.

Perched on the edge of the seat, Beth took a long breath and her words came out in a rush as she exhaled.

"I am going to have a baby, Kristen! Can you believe it? Me—going to be a mother!"

"Oh, Beth, I'm so glad for you—and for Brian. But when?"

"The doctor said sometime in May."

151

Kristen laughed. "And I don't suppose Brian's excited."

"Not much, he isn't!" she said smugly. "He's so careful of me and worries so when I'm sick in the mornings."

"Are you very sick in the mornings?"

"Marvelously!" Beth said with satisfaction and Kristen had to laugh again. Beth was so thrilled with the prospect of motherhood she could even enjoy morning sickness.

Then she looked at Beth with apprehension, for her knowledge of pregnancies was scant at best.

"Should you be traveling?"

Beth smiled and said, with the expert knowledge of a woman who has had her pregnancy confirmed for one whole week, "Oh, that's why I flew. Brian wouldn't hear of my driving alone and I just had to tell Aunt Maude and Uncle Frank in person. Besides, I'm healthy as a horse."

She closed her eyes and laid her head back on the seat, smiling somewhat smugly to herself. Watching her, Kristen felt a pang of resentment which she immediately stiffled. It certainly was not Beth's fault her affairs were in such wretched shape; she had only herself to blame for that. Beth would certainly never fight against her feelings and emotions as she had done. Beth would have relaxed, smiled, and opened her arms to them.

At least, Kristen thought hopefully, Beth was so wound up in her new development her shrewd sisterly eyes would not notice anything different about her sister.

But Kristen was mistaken. No happiness, however great, ever clouded Beth's vision as far as her sister was concerned. Scatterbrained Beth might be, but she was always very discerning about those she loved, especially Kristen.

So it was while Kristen was preparing for bed that night that there was a perfunctory knock on her door and Beth slipped into the room. This same ritual had been performed hundreds of times throughout their growing-up years: Beth coming into Kristen's room, or the other way around, to talk before going to bed. Many problems had been solved, many decisions reached during this time.

And if Kristen had thought her sister had come in to discuss her enlarging family, she soon dismissed this thought; obviously something entirely different was on her mind. She came in and propped herself up on the pillows and lay quietly watching as her sister slipped into her nightgown.

Beth sat up, pulled her knees up, rested her chin, and frowned, perplexed. "I don't know what it is, Kris, but I do know there's something the matter. You're not happy about something. No, don't start denying it," she said impatiently. "I didn't come in here to listen to a bunch of denials. I could tell at supper something was wrong and I want to know what it is. And furthermore, I fully intend to stay right here"—she pounded the bed with a stubborn forefinger—"until you tell me exactly what it is. So save us both some time and get started."

Having issued her ultimatum, she sank back onto the pillows again and waited. Kristen frowned and stood staring, irresolute, at her sister. She meant exactly what she said. She would remain until she knew. Not out of curiosity but out of a deep-seated concern.

Kristen walked over and sat down on the bed; her fingers plucked idly, then nervously, at the fluff of the bedspread.

"Do you remember Clay Courtney?" she asked finally. "He was the man we met—"

"Oh, I remember him right enough," Beth interrupted. "He isn't exactly the type one's likely to forget in a hurry. Do you mean you've seen him again?"

Beth sat up again, instantly engrossed, and Kristen began, hesitantly at first, but as she talked she found she was telling Beth everything: about Clay's overbearing arrogance, his demands, though, in all fairness to him, she did not fail to admit that there had been tender moments, many of them, and that he had said he loved her; about how she had reacted toward him, and her indecision about Roger.

"Why can't I be like you, Beth?" she asked when she had finally finished. "You don't question things, you just open your heart and accept them."

Beth shook her head. "You'll never be like me, Kristen," she said, smiling. "You're too brainy." Then she sobered and the smile disappeared. "Would you mind some sisterly advice, for what it's worth?"

Kristen threw her a despairing look. "I'd be delighted with some," she assured her.

"Well, here it is. First off, you've got to admit to yourself that you ran away from him—and that's exactly what you did, you know. You ran away because he was more than you were able to handle. You've always called the shots before and Roger, and all the others before him, fell into line. But Clay is different. He called a few of the shots and you didn't like it, or at least you told yourself you didn't. Deep down you're probably crazy about it, and him, and just won't admit it. Do you actually believe you could be happy spending the rest of your life with some dry-as-dust like Roger after knowing someone like Clay? Where would be the challenge? Not you—you need someone who's strong, who will give you that challenge and yet be able to stand by you or to support you when you need it. Don't kid yourself anymore, Kris," she said softly, leaning forward to put her hand on her sister's arm. "Just learn to give a little—that's all he's asking. And if you love him, it won't be too difficult, believe me."

Kristen felt the prick of tears forming behind her eyelids; she shook her head despairingly. "It's good advice, Beth, but I'm afraid it's come a little too late. He's gone back to his ranch and this time I'm quite sure he isn't coming back."

To mumble platitudes or meaningless suppositions at a time like this would be less than worthless, so there was nothing left for Beth to say.

CHAPTER 19

It was during the next morning that Roger came. Beth showed him into Uncle Frank's study and then went in search of Kristen. She found her, after a time, in the attic, listlessly going through old dust-covered boxes.

"Whatever are you doing up here, Kris?" Beth asked, her eyes taking in the masses of junk that had been packed away long ago and now lay about in heaps on the floor. Kristen could not very well tell her she had retreated to the attic in hopes of being alone for a while; although Beth would probably have understood, she might have been hurt at the same time.

"I didn't have anything else to do," Kristen explained with a shrug, "and you know how I am about attics. I thought I'd look through some of our old stuff. It's all here."

Beth laughed and pulled up a stool and squatted on it. "Oh, look, my old senior album from high school. Man!" she said with horror as she flipped to a page and looked closely, "I was a regular freak! Look at that hair-do. Why, that's right out of the Middle Ages."

Kristen grinned. "I know. I just found a snapshot of me in a bathing suit—nothing but skin and bones. But I'm sure at the time I thought I looked great."

Beth laid the album aside and began to dig around in a nearby trunk, exclaiming over each item she dug to light.

". . . and here's that old scrapbook of movie clippings

I used to collect back in junior high. Aunt Maude certainly doesn't throw away much. And here's that picture I had made when we went on that band tour, remember?" She stopped suddenly. "Oh, good grief, Roger!"

Kristen leaned forward to see what she was looking at.

"No, not here—downstairs! He's waiting for you in Uncle Frank's study. I forgot all about him."

Kristen got to her feet, dusting the seat of her slacks. "I'd better go down," she said, looking at Beth, who was still pulling items from the trunk. "You coming?"

Beth glanced up over her shoulder. "He didn't come to see me, Kristen. He came to see you and I'm sure you know why. You're going to have to come to a decision about Roger, you know. It isn't fair not to. After all, he has his life ahead of him too."

Walking slowly down the stairs, Kristen thought over what Beth had said. She was right, of course. If she didn't intend to marry Roger, she would have to tell him so. She opened the door and stepped into the study, closing the door behind her.

"Hello, Roger," she said quietly. "I'm sorry to have kept you waiting, but I was up in the attic and Beth had a hard time finding me. I'm afraid I must look an awful mess."

Roger, standing across the room by the window, did not say it, but he was sure she had never looked lovelier. Her dark hair was tousled about her face as it was apt to be when left alone; a streak of dust lay on her cheek, and although her face did not have its usual color, it only made her eyes appear even larger and more brilliantly blue.

Walking to her, he placed his hands gently on her shoulders; he bent his head to brush his lips lightly against her cheek. Then he stepped back. He seemed to sense some change in her, some restraint.

"How have you been, Kristen?" he asked, watching her closely.

Kristen avoided his eyes. "I've been fine, Roger. Very busy, as you know." She turned from him suddenly and walked to the window. "Roger, I have to tell you—"

"Wait a moment," he interrupted, taking a quick step forward.

Kristen swung around to face him, to try to stop him from saying anything. Even with Roger things were getting out of hand. "Roger," she repeated, but still he would not let her finish.

"No, let me say it, Kristen. It isn't my intention, never has been, to force myself on you or to try to coerce you into any decision on my behalf. You know how I feel about you. How I've always felt. But I'll not make any demands. I just thought I might . . . that we might . . ." He caught the look in her eye and was silent.

She dropped her eyes and a deep sigh shook her. *Doesn't he know I don't want to be apologized to, that he might possibly get further if he stopped being so apologetic and just took me in his arms and kissed me? But no, he wouldn't do that, wouldn't even think of it—and what's more to the point, he wouldn't have any way of knowing that might be what I wanted. I never desired that sort of treatment before.*

"You mean it, don't you, Kristen?" he said quietly. "I mean, there's really nothing between us. Up to now I thought there was a chance, but now something's different. You've changed somehow since the last time we were together."

Kristen looked up. "And as far as you're concerned, that's that?" she asked.

Roger laughed shortly. "It wouldn't do for me to press you. I'd certainly get nowhere that way. If you don't mind my saying so, you can be fairly strong-willed sometimes and you've never taken kindly to anyone telling you what to do."

"But couldn't you have tried forcing the issue, just this once?"

Roger was frankly puzzled; he shook his head. "I don't understand all this, Kristen. Either you want me or you don't. I—"

She took his hand, pressed it, and then released it. "I want to apologize, Roger. I was just trying to work something out in my mind—which I've been told is one of my failings. I am sorry, for everything."

She stood gazing, unseeing, out the window for a long time after he had gone. She put her head against the windowpane and the tears, held back for so long, slid slowly down her cheeks.

With a tact unusual for her Beth suggested during lunch that Kristen might like to go to town after she had finished eating and do a little shopping.

"I'm sure with her work she has little enough time to browse around the shops," she explained, "and it's always harder to find what you want in a strange city."

Kristen gave her a grateful look; she needed to get out for a while by herself. Maybe take a long drive and then lose the long afternoon wandering through the shops. Yes, that would be a godsend.

Then, with a sinking feeling, she heard Uncle Frank saying he would be going down to the store after lunch and he could drive her down and after she had finished her shopping, she could come to the store and he would drive her home. Beth's eyes met Kristen's and she shrugged her shoulders in a helpless gesture.

Kristen was about to accept the offer resignedly when, surprisingly enough, Aunt Maude came to her rescue.

"Shouldn't you get your car out and drive it some, Kristen?" she put in mildly. "Except for that short run to the airport, it's been locked in the garage. I've never understood exactly why, but your uncle is always saying that a car should be driven regularly. Isn't that so, Frank?"

Frank nodded his agreement, but before he could say that Kristen's car had hardly been parked that long, Kristen put in quickly: "Yes, I guess you're right, Uncle Frank. I'd better drive my car. And I do need to get some gasoline anyway, but thanks for the offer."

After lunch and before anything could deter her, she grabbed her purse and went out the front door, and out to the garage. She drove to the service station, made light conversation with the boy at the pump, and then drove awhile around the country roads. Her mind was riddled with thoughts, but she could come to no conclusions whatsoever, so she gave it up and headed back to town.

She maneuvered into a parking space on the main street and proceeded on her way down the street, but as it turned out, the shopping trip proved to be a failure. She found nothing interesting enough to purchase, mainly because her interests kept wandering; she kept running into old friends and acquaintances, mostly students from the college who would have been her classmates had she not taken the position as Mrs. Faraday's assistant but returned to classes in the fall, who spoke of people and talked of events that did not concern her. This served to give her a strange, detached feeling of not belonging anymore.

Finally she put aside the sweater in which she had been pretending an interest and walked out of the shop, smiling automatically at the clerk, who called her by name. Wishing she were back in impersonal San Antonio where she didn't have to keep smiling at people, acknowledging greetings, she walked down the block to the corner and stood waiting for the light to change. She was paying no attention to the cars passing until one stopped suddenly directly in front of her and the driver leaned across the seat and opened the door.

"Get in," was the terse command and Kristen's eyes focused quickly on the driver. He was looking at her through the open door and from the look in his eyes she knew he would brook no argument and he was holding up traffic and the familiar eyes around her were starting to stare. She climbed in quickly and shut the door as he moved the car into the stream of traffic.

"Where can we go to talk?" he asked without looking at her.

Kristen cast an oblique glance at his face, noted the firm set of his jaw, and moved a little more into her corner.

"Clay, I—"

"I said, where can we go to talk? Somewhere where there's no people and we won't be disturbed."

She took a deep breath that shook as she released it. "This street runs into the highway after you pass the college. I'll show you where to turn off of the highway."

They rode on in a heavy silence until they came to an unpaved road leading off the highway. "If you turn here" —she pointed—"and drive for a short way, there's another smaller road leading to an old mill. It's deserted now; no one ever goes there."

There was more of the same tense silence until they came to the mill; Clay drove around to the back and stopped. Kristen had not seen him quite so intense; he sat now regarding her with such intensity she wanted to squirm.

Finally she could stand it no longer; he did not seem inclined to speak, but something had to be done to break the impossible silence and to stop him from looking at her.

"How did you know where to find me?" she asked quietly.

"It wasn't too difficult—once I decided I wanted to."

There was something in his words that made her wince.

"Why did you decide you wanted to?" she found herself asking, her voice barely audible.

"I don't know," he ground out between his teeth. "I must be flat out crazy. I thought the last time I saw you

161

I was really through. And then I find myself chasing over half the state looking for you. Man!"

She leaned toward him slightly. "Clay, listen to me, please. I—"

He turned back and nailed her with a thunderous scowl. "No, this time you're going to listen to me. And I've got quite a lot to say, so you just sit tight and don't interrupt me.

"When I first left San Antonio, I went back to the ranch with the fool thought that we were finally getting somewhere, you and me. And how I missed you! But there was a lot of work to be done when I got back because things had gotten behind with just Shorty to do the work. We had a couple of hands working for us, but they decided they were needed back in their homeland and that left us short-handed.

"I thought about you, when I wasn't dead on my feet. I thought about calling you, but by the time the day's work was behind us, it would be too late, and talking on the phone wasn't quite enough. So I'd just fall into the bed and would have just enough time to think of you before I fell asleep."

Kristen made a sound as if to speak, but a raised eyebrow silenced her.

"We finally got caught up around the place and the wandering vaqueros had returned, so I decided, like a complete idiot, that I'd like to see you again and that I could probably take some time off if I didn't stretch it too far. Shorty was glad to see me go; he's put up with a lot from me over the past days.

"And what did I find? That you were still holding me at arm's length while you decided if you wanted me, or someone else, or no one. So I lost my temper and went back home. And I worked like the very devil trying to forget you. Every time I found myself remembering you, I'd tell myself to think about all the times you told me,

162

coolly and calmly, that we weren't suited. And for a while I fooled myself into believing it. But it just didn't work. You see, I can't tell myself these things, lie to myself and make myself believe it the way you seem to be able to do. The problem I have is that I'm every inch as stubborn and hardheaded as you are—only more so, and when I want something as badly as I wanted you, it was next to impossible to deny myself. You've said it—I'm arrogant, selfish, and all the rest."

He paused a moment and then went on.

"So I decided to give it one more try. I went to San Antonio only to find you'd gone home. Mrs. Faraday told me how to find you and wished me luck. I went to your uncle's house and your aunt told me you were in town shopping and where I'd probably find you."

When he finished, he reached out and clasped his hands tightly about her arms, bringing her close to him until his face was above hers. The anger was gone from his eyes, but there was a tightness about his mouth and the eyes, cool and assessing, held hers. His voice was low and even.

"Now, look at me, Kristen, and tell me I was wrong—tell me you don't love me. Tell me you'd rather have someone else. Tell me this one last time and I'll leave you alone and stop bothering you. But don't," he warned her, "don't tell me what you've thought out with your mind. Tell me what you feel inside. If you don't want me, then say it, but don't lie to me, sweetheart, and don't lie to yourself."

Kristen's hands shook as she laid them on his chest and her lips trembled, but her eyes never wavered. "I've quit lying to myself, Clay," she whispered. "I can't say I don't love you because I do—I love you very much. I didn't intend to. I didn't want to because you seemed to demand more of me than I was willing to give, but I see now that's the way it has to be with you—with us. It has to be everything or nothing. I'm not exactly sure when it happened. I only know the last few days have been thoroughly wretched for me."

She looked at him desperately, wishing he would take her into his arms, but he only sat looking at her, forcing her by his silence and his immobility to continue.

"And as for being cold," she went on, "do you have even the remotest idea of the amount of restraint I've had to use where you're concerned? I've never had my feelings react as violently as they do when I'm with you and it's been a totally new experience for me." She looked at him. "How much more do you want me to say?"

His arms went around her, pulling her close to him. "That's all. But you had to say it, for yourself as much as for me. It hasn't been easy for you—"

She put a finger up to his lips, stopping his words. "Clay, please, don't say any more. Just kiss me."

His arms tightened. "You're right. There's been too much talk."

She relaxed in his arms, giving herself to his embrace; her lips moved beneath his in a way they never had before, her body yielding to the demands of his touch without restraint.

"I love you, Kristen, and I want you so much," he murmured.

"I know, Clay, I know," she answered, her voice faltering.

His whispered words became more passionate as his desire to possess her mounted swiftly. She could feel her body slipping downward as the weight of his pressed upon her and she opened her arms to him, ready now to give herself to him, to lose herself in him completely.

But it was Clay who stopped suddenly and with a quick movement pulled himself up; then he lifted Kristen up beside him and cradled her in his arms.

"Clay?" she said after a moment, looking at him in

bewilderment. "What is it? Did I do something wrong? I was only—"

He laughed rather shakily and brushed his hand across his eyes. She noticed that his hand was shaking.

"You didn't do anything wrong, honey," he assured her emphatically. "Believe me, you were doing just fine. It's just that"—he turned to take her face in both his hands— "it's just that even though I've wanted you for such a long time, Kristen, I can't stand the idea of taking you here, in the front seat of a parked car. It has all the undertones of dirt and I love you too much for that. Now you can call me a fool—I sure feel like one."

She let out a long sigh and closed her eyes briefly. "I thought it was me. That you found you didn't want me after all."

Clay kissed her lightly. "I found I wanted you even more than ever, but there's got to be more to it; it's got to go deeper."

Kristen turned to look at him. "Is that a proposal?"

"If it is, what's your answer?"

Her smile was brilliant. "Yes, of course."

"Well, let me warn you, it's going to have to be fast, before my resolve runs out. Where you're concerned my resolve is a fairly weak commodity."

He leaned to kiss her again, but she pulled back. "I thought you told me you couldn't make love in a car, but you seemed fairly capable to me just now."

He grinned. "That's because you've not had enough experience to really judge. And as I recall, I didn't say that I couldn't—I just said that I hadn't mastered it." Glancing at the darkening sky and then at his watch, he said, "I'd better get you home."

She sighed.

"I know how you feel, Kristen. Believe me, I know. But this is the way it's got to be."

Kristen felt her face growing warm. "Clay, I didn't

165

". . . I don't want . . . "

Clay laughed softly. "You're lying to yourself again," he admonished her.

She opened her purse hurriedly and began combing her hair while Clay backed the car onto the road.

"You know, your Aunt Maude is a fine woman," he said as they drove along the highway, "and intelligent too."

"How so?" she inquired.

"When I said I was looking for you and she told me where to find you, she said something else. She said, 'Well, now maybe Kristen will be her old self again.' She gave you away, sweetheart."

Kristen cocked her head sideways and pondered this. "I guess I've always underestimated Aunt Maude," she decided.

"And Beth," Clay continued, "she looked like the cat with the cream." He paused. "Oh, I also met up with Roger."

Kristen's eyes widened. "Roger?" she said. "Where?"

"At your house. He had come to get something for the store and your aunt introduced me as a friend of yours. He looked a little ill and I don't think he cared too much for me."

She refrained from asking any questions about how he felt, but the silence that followed spoke volumes.

They were pulling into the driveway before Kristen recalled her car was still parked downtown.

"It's all right. I'll take you down later. I made such a favorable impression on your family I was invited back to dinner."

CHAPTER 20

For Kristen the evening meal went on in a haze around her. She ate, she talked, she answered hundreds of questions, but her voice sounded strange to her ears; she listened to the talk but heard little of the actual words. She found herself staring at the familiar face across the table and thinking how odd it was to have him there. She had gone to town a very mixed up and terribly unhappy woman and had returned with a man, a man who would in time be her husband. She felt in a daze; it was all so unreal.

But Clay, she thought with some asperity, seemed to be taking it all in his stride; he was obviously enjoying his meal immensely, to Aunt Maude's delight. She was constantly plying him with food, exclaiming mildly that he could use some filling out. And he was replying, almost pitifully, that Shorty's cooking did leave a lot to be desired and Aunt Maude was lapping it up. Did women ever get too old for him not to try to charm them? Recalling how he had dazzled Mrs. Faraday, she decided they did not.

It had been decided during the course of the meal that Clay would remain in Marshalton overnight and then both he and Kristen would return to San Antonio the next day, Clay following in his car.

"I'll take Kristen down to get her car and she can direct me to a good motel," Clay stated. "Less trouble that way."

Seeing he could not be swayed from his decision, Aunt

167

Maude extracted his promise that he would come for breakfast, which he gave readily enough.

After dinner Kristen directed him to one of the newer motels, a large sprawling affair with multicolored doors, and waited in the car until he returned.

"Trust me enough to come in for a little while?" he asked and Kristen shook her head.

"Oh, I trust you well enough, but as well as I'm known in this town, it would be all over the place in less than an hour that Kristen Ames had been seen going into a motel with a man. No, thanks."

Clay shook his head. "Poor Roger. Now I know what he was up against. How can you make time with a girl with the whole town watching over your shoulder?"

It was not late, but the stores, except for a restaurant or two, had closed and the streets were already practically deserted. Kristen's car was one of about half a dozen still parked along the street.

Clay pulled to the curb behind it and switched off the motor. "I guess if I kissed you now half the town would know it by eleven o'clock, wouldn't they?"

She leaned toward him, slipping her arms about his waist, and turned her face up to his. "It won't bother me if it won't bother you."

It was a long kiss, but soft, filled with a gentle promise; there was no need now for urgency or demand.

"Come on, sweetheart," he said softly, "it's to your car with you. The gossips will be standing on their ears."

After she had moved in under the wheel, he leaned to kiss her lightly, murmuring a good night, and went back to his car. He waited until she had pulled away and then he turned back in the direction of the motel. He toyed for a moment with the idea of stopping in the coffee shop and then decided in favor of his room and bed.

But he was restless and spent the better part of an hour pacing his room. He thought of Kristen with satisfaction, feeling that everything had gone well enough. She was his now—wasn't she?

And that was the question that kept nagging at him. His meeting with her had been somewhat of an anticlimax, leaving him dissatisfied and a little uneasy.

With an angry gesture he began stripping off his clothes. The best thing for him to do was to get to sleep and quit thinking because his thoughts were only serving to make him more restless. He was cursing himself roundly when he finally dropped off to sleep.

CHAPTER 21

"But, Clay, it's impossible for us to get married tomorrow," she told him again and Clay ground his teeth. She winced, knowing he resented her telling him that something he wanted badly was impossible.

"Clay," she ventured, trying to get him to see reason, "you know as well as I do that it takes three days in Texas. There's the blood tests—"

He flipped his cigarette into the fireplace with an angry gesture. "I know," he interrupted impatiently, "or at least I should by now—you've certainly told me enough times."

"Clay, it isn't that I don't want to marry you right away. It's just that it's—"

"I know. It's impossible!"

Due to his past experiences with Kristen, during the restless night Clay had been almost obsessed with the thought that they should be married immediately. He had finally admitted to himself that he was apprehensive that she might revert to her old way of thinking and change her mind, pushing him away as she had done so many times in the past.

To get his mind off this new idea Kristen asked, "Do you mind if we go back to San Antonio as soon after breakfast as we can get away? Although that isn't going to be easily done. Aunt Maude and Uncle Frank won't like my leaving this soon."

Suddenly Clay's eyes brightened. "You know, I think maybe getting to San Antonio right away just might be the best idea after all. I believe Mrs. Faraday is a very resourceful woman when she wants to be and when the need arises—and I've sure got the need."

Kristen eyed him, puzzled. "Whatever are you talking about? What possible need do you have that Mrs. Faraday might be able to help you with?"

He actually laughed and she stared at him, for he had not so much as smiled since he had arrived that morning. "I have an overpowering need to get married and I think Mrs. Faraday just might have the answer to our problems."

They arrived at the Faraday house to find everything in a state of confusion. Mrs. Faraday, sitting on one of the couches in what could only be termed a calm repose while she directed Ramon in the moving about of the furniture, which was no easy job due to the lack of available space in which to move.

When Kristen and Clay stepped into the room, Mrs. Faraday's eyes brightened with pleasure and Ramon looked around with relief. She got to her feet, forgetting completely the presence of all the clutter around her.

"Kristen, how glad I am to see you back." She took Kristen's hands in hers and pressed them firmly. Glancing up at Clay, she added, "We've been having a little difficulty here, you know." She looked around at the chaos surrounding them and sought to explain. "I thought I'd take this opportunity to try moving things around to make more room." She shook her head despairingly. "But it does seem an impossible job. You can go along now, Ramon." The man escaped with obvious relief.

She motioned for them to be seated, took a deep breath, and then leaned forward to look at Kristen more closely.

171

"Are you sure you're all right, dear? You looked strained before you left."

Kristen patted the woman gently on the arm. "I'm fine, Mrs. Faraday. But what about yourself? You look a bit tired."

"Tut, child, I've never been better." Then her eyes narrowed. "But you two are up to something—I can tell. So out with it."

She had addressed the question to Kristen, but her eyes slid around to Clay. Kristen turned to look up at him and noticed that the grim lines were again firmly etched around his mouth and his eyes.

"We intend to get married, and today if it can be arranged." His eyes studied her carefully and he was sure that he had detected just the faintest flicker of an idea pass across her face. "Do you think it's possible? Can it be done?" he asked, but Kristen broke in.

"I've been telling him it's just impossible. There's the blood tests—"

She never seemed to be able to complete that sentence before Clay managed to silence her. This time he accomplished it by using a sternly raised eyebrow. He did not have three days to waste. He could take the time away from the ranch to get married, but not to sit around and wait. And he refused to leave Kristen alone. In the back of his mind remained that growing doubt. He still hated to admit it, but it was there. Would Kristen start thinking again and decide she didn't want him after all. Man! He hated to admit it!

"I've been thinking," Mrs. Faraday said quietly and Clay swung to face her. "I've been thinking that, as I recall, there's no waiting period in New Mexico."

Kristen regarded her with amazement. "How did you come by that bit of information?"

Mrs. Faraday shrugged. "Oh, a person just picks up things of that sort in conversation," she said airily. "And while I was there, I met this marvelous young preacher. His church is small, mostly Indians, I think. Quaint and colorful—not too far from the state line."

Kristen smiled indulgently. "It all sounds delightful, Mrs. Faraday, but we couldn't think of driving to New Mexico. . . ."

Her voice trailed away as she glanced up at Clay, fully expecting him to think the idea as preposterous as she did, and was startled by the look in his eyes.

"Clay?" she asked cautiously. "What are you thinking?"

The old twinkle had returned; his smile warmed her. "You know exactly what I'm thinking, sweetheart." Then he turned to Mrs. Faraday. "Now, if you've got a road map handy, I think we're in business."

CHAPTER 22

"I think we both must be crazy," Kristen stated firmly as they sped down the highway in the middle of the night.

Clay laughed and hugged her close. "Mrs. Faraday thought it was a grand idea," he defended himself.

"And Mrs. Faraday is as crazy are you are," she retorted. "And all this speeding through the night to get married is right up her romantic alley."

Clay looked pleased. "I told you the old girl could do it."

"I should say she did! She had the state, the church, and the preacher—only thing she lacked was the license in her pocket."

"I wish she'd had that—it would have saved us some time," Clay said thoughtfully.

Her eyes widened; she shook her head despairingly. "Don't you think this rushing around to get married in such a hurry is just the least bit obscene?"

"Obscene? Here I am breaking the speed limit trying to keep you an honest woman, and you call it obscene!"

She laughed. "Well, I must say it'll be a marriage I'm not likely to forget."

Clay's arm about her waist tightened suddenly. "Are you sorry we're doing it this way, Kristen? With no big church wedding and all that?"

He had slackened his speed and was looking at her with a troubled frown. Was she sorry? he asked himself guiltily, for he had not given her a chance to say if she had wanted it this way or not. He had been so delighted with the idea, glad to be doing something, but she was a woman and it mattered to a woman how these things were done. Had the doubts he had been having about her caused him to rush into something too quickly?

"Are you sorry, honey?" he asked again, urgently now.

She put her hand to his cheek. "No, of course I'm not sorry, Clay."

He continued to study her until he was satisfied that she was really telling him the truth and not just trying to make the best of a bad bargain, then turned his full attention back to his driving.

They had no trouble locating the small church; the young preacher, a trifle startled, was as marvelous as stated to be and his church was quaint and colorful. The ceremony was conducted with a simple, unhurried and quiet dignity. When it was finished, there were tears on Kristen's lashes, but she was pleased with everything; Clay, watching her, looked greatly relieved.

They said their good-byes to the preacher and then spent the remainder of the day driving to Santa Fe, where Clay had decided they would spend the next few days in the nearby mountains.

He had telephoned ahead and their room was ready when they arrived and a short while later Kristen found herself standing, irresolute, in the center of a large room looking across to where Clay was standing watching her.

It was quiet and neither spoke. They had driven all night and most of the day, events had moved with startling rapidity that left her more than a little confused. And now they were here. And she was appalled to find that she was nervous and more than a little apprehensive of this man, her husband, who was now alone with her in this strange room.

Sensing her nervousness and again feeling his own

doubts and alarms over just how she might react, Clay tried to smile reassuringly.

"It's really all right, you know. We *are* married."

She glanced down at the hastily bought gold band on her finger as if she wondered just how it had got to be there. "I know, but it was all so fast—it seems unreal."

He was fighting down a growing sense of panic. "It's almost time for dinner," he said across the space that still divided them, seeking to keep his voice calm. He was afraid to move, afraid she might . . . do what? "Would you like to go down or would you rather have something sent up?"

She shook her head. "I'm really not hungry." Her voice shook slightly and she sought to steady it. She took a long breath before adding, "But we'll do whatever you want."

For a long moment he did not speak; his eyes sought hers, caught and held them. "You know what I want, Kristen," he said, his voice suddenly soft, barely audible across the room. The words had been spoken before he fully realized what he had said. Now he waited, tensed for her reaction.

His words caused her breath to catch. Yes, she knew what he wanted, what he had always wanted from her. But she could find no words to answer him.

Then he smiled. "But I can wait," he said. His eyes were burning, but he strove to keep his voice light. "It isn't even dark yet."

Quite plainly now it was up to her. He was waiting for her, as he had been waiting for her all along. No doubt he was afraid she had shut him out again, had changed her mind as she had done so often in the past.

"It wasn't dark that time behind the mill," she heard herself saying, "but that wasn't what stopped you then. I'd say you've run out of excuses."

His eyes blazed suddenly and he took a step toward her. But something inside her rebelled at his movement. She did not want it this way, with all the embarrassment and uncertainty of his hands fumbling about with buttons and zippers. Surely it could be handled in a better way, in a way that would make her feel more a wife and a woman loved and not just another quick time passed in a hotel room.

To halt his movement she held up both hands, palms out. "Please, Clay, wait," she said quickly and he checked his stride. His eyebrows dipped into a sudden frown. His eyes narrowed. Just what sort of game was she playing? "Please, would you leave me?" she asked and she saw his eyebrows lift questioningly. "Would you go somewhere and leave me alone for just a few minutes—just this once?"

He felt a cold jab of apprehension. Would she use this time to talk herself into the notion that she had made a mistake? She was very good at that.

"How long do you want me to stay away?"

"Not long—ten minutes."

Ten minutes. She couldn't do much thinking in ten minutes. He grinned, breaking the tension. "I'll give you ten minutes—but not a second more," he warned her and left the room.

And in ten minutes she heard him at the door, but now she was ready for him. In the short time allowed her she had brushed her hair until it fell about her shoulders in dark waves; she had discarded her dress and had slipped into a soft, sheer gown of white lace and was now propped up on the pillows, ready to meet him, her nervousness a thing of the past.

He stepped into the room and in the waning light saw her waiting for him. Slowly but without hesitation she held out her arms to him and slowly he went to her.

With unhurried movements, his eyes never leaving hers, his fingers worked at the buttons of his shirt. He felt a great sense of relief, coupled with a surging expectancy, that she had not been putting him off but had been prepar-

177

ing a more proper setting for the sharing of their love. He felt his love for her growing as he divested himself of the last of his clothing and moved to lie beside her.

She, in turn, had been very aware of him as he had come through the twilit room toward her, and now she felt a surge of the same expectancy and not a little pride in this man who moved with such purpose toward her.

She lay looking up at him, her hair spreading out on the pillow, her eyes watching him, brilliantly blue. His face, close to her now, seemed to blaze with a deep, golden warmth that spread over her. He moved closer to her and she felt the soft smoothness of her gown sliding from her and being replaced by the firm hardness of his hands. His touch, the strange, new feeling of a man's hands caressing her, brought from the depths within her responses she had not realized she possessed. The reality of him, of his body pressed firmly to hers brought new sensations, which seemed to quicken something deep inside her; his kisses, growing stronger as his needs increased, the workings of his hands—all were bringing her more fully alive than she had ever been, and she knew it pleasured him that he was able to do this for her.

"Kristen," his deep voice whispered, muffled at her ear, "sweetheart, I didn't know I could feel this way—that I could feel this strongly about anyone."

Before he had spoken the words, she had known, even in her inexperience, that whatever previous experiences he had had, her love and her open response to him were bringing to him a more beautiful and a deeper meaning than he had ever believed possible.

"I know, Clay," she whispered, "I know."

And now her hands came alive, exploring, discovering, learning through touch all there was to know of this new being who was soon to be a part of her own. Her fingers moved along hard, firm thighs, across narrow hips, up the broad expanse of his back and pressed themselves there, holding him close to her as he prepared her for the moment when they would become as one.

In that moment his eyes sought hers, his gaze penetrating, searching, questioning. "You aren't afraid, are you, Kristen?" he asked with true concern. "I don't want you to be afraid, not of me."

Her eyes never wavered and her body moved to his, giving him the assurance that he needed. He heard her words, her lips soft at his ear.

"I'm not afraid, Clay. Not of you. Not ever."

"I love you, Kristen," he murmured, his lips pressed against her hair. He wasn't sure he had said it. He wanted to say it.

The room was dark now and they had gone to stand by the large window that opened out onto the night around them. It had begun to snow in the mountains. A light, airy powdering shone below them like silver in the night. It was a fairyland and Kristen felt as if she were a part of it. She could almost feel the snowflakes in some sensous way touching her skin.

A shiver rippled through her, not from cold but from pure delight in the ecstasy of all that had happened to her.

"Are you cold, sweetheart?" He pulled her closer to him, his hands, his arms closing tighter about her. "Do you want your robe, your gown?"

She could hear the regret in his words and knew he wanted to go on feeling her next to him, her body touching his.

Kristen sighed with contentment, putting her arms around him, pressing against him. "No, I'm fine, Clay, and I don't need anything but you."

"And you're mine now," she heard him say with fierce pride, "all mine."

Her arms tightened around him, marveling at the firm strength of him. "And you are mine." There was a note of wonder in her voice. She was wondering too why she had fought so hard against such completeness.

Clay leaned back to look down at her.

"There were times I wasn't sure I'd ever get you here. And I'll admit I was afraid that if I ever did, you'd freeze up on me. You gave me a few shaky moments, but"—his arm tightened, the other hand tilting her face up to his—"I was wrong. And you're still not sorry?" he asked, lowering his head to nestle his face in the hollow of her throat.

"No, I'm not sorry," she said simply, for her throat would not allow further speech.

As his mouth once again moved to cover hers, blocking out all possibility of further conversation, the cold of the snowflakes outside the window was dispelled by the warmth of his kiss, the love they shared.

CHAPTER 23

Clay, assured now that Kristen loved him with a completeness equal to his own, still had one reservation left that was keeping him from total happiness. How would Kristen, formerly so involved in her work with Mrs. Faraday and so determined to devote herself to her further studies, fit into life as the wife of a rancher?

The next morning the thought first began to plague him. It was early when he awoke. He had been waking up early all his life, especially during these last years, and it was a habit he found difficult to break. So, although the night had brought little sleep, he found himself wide awake even before the first fingers of dawn moved over the surrounding mountains. And he found himself faced with this new thought.

As he lay beside Kristen, feeling her softness against him, stirrings of need for her once again began to build in him. Looking down at her sleeping soundly and knowing she doubtless needed this rest, he pushed his desire resolutely from him. But he knew he could not remain beside her and not want to make love to her; therefore, he eased out of the bed so as not to awaken her and went to stand by the window where the two of them had stood just a short time earlier. Now he watched the sun slowly turn the eastern sky to an early morning pink.

The snow, a caprice of autumn in the mountains, had

disappeared, but he knew there would be a nip in the air. Even so, it would be warm still at the ranch.

The ranch.

Now he felt his earlier uneasiness once again. He began to wrestle with it, to reason.

She had liked the out of doors—hadn't he met her while she was on a camping trip? And she had said she liked horses—or had she? He really couldn't remember what she had said. He had been so busy talking that he hadn't really listened.

But she wouldn't have married him, a rancher, if she hadn't wanted to be a rancher's wife, would she? But what did she know of ranch life?

His lips twisted in self-derision. Had he really given her much of an opportunity to tell him how she felt about that part of their life? No, he had kept at her with everything he had until she had given in to him completely. He had wanted her and that had been as far as he had thought.

He ran a distracted hand through his hair, once again feeling as if he were no longer in control, and despising the feeling.

He needed a cup of coffee, he decided, and glancing back at the sleeping figure on the bed, he knew coffee was a poor substitute for what he truly wanted. But for the moment it would have to suffice.

With more resolution he passed by the bed and went searching about for his clothes.

"Clay?"

He jerked around quickly to see Kristen sitting up watching him with a puzzled frown, shamelessly letting the covers fall away, her skin touched by the rose of the dawn as she brushed her hair back from where it had fallen loosely about her shoulders. Desire flamed up in him.

"Clay," she repeated, as he appeared unable to move,

watching her, "why are you getting dressed? Isn't it awfully early?"

Finally he began moving toward her, dropping clothing in his wake.

"Much too early, sweetheart," he assured her and once again she was in his arms.

The night before he had thought her desirable when he had found her waiting for him; he had found her desirable as they had watched the snowflakes in the night. Now in the early dawn he found, looking down into her eyes, still more asleep than awake, with her hair tousled about and her voice slightly thickened with sleep, that she was even more desirable.

"You were leaving," she said accusingly as she snuggled into his embrace.

"Only because you were asleep," he assured her, his voice light, "and I certainly wasn't going far."

"If I had slept a few moments longer, I would have woken up and you would have been gone." Her eyes opened wider at the thought.

He smiled down at her and his mouth moved to cover hers.

Later, as he sat on the bed watching as she came out of the shower draped in a towel, he again felt vague misgivings. As the towel dropped and she began looking about for her underthings, he started to speak as he moved toward the shower.

"I thought I'd give Shorty a call, see how things are going at the ranch."

He watched her covertly to see her reaction.

"That's a good idea," she responded in an offhanded manner as she fastened her bra with a practiced hand that he could not help but admire. He never could understand how women accomplished that particular feat.

He forced himself back to the problem at hand, frowning. He didn't seem to be learning much.

"I went off kinda sudden like. He might be having some trouble."

Sensing a different sound to his voice, she turned to look at him. "Do you think you, or rather we, should go back?"

He stopped short. "Would you mind?"

"Of course not." She smiled at him. "It was your wild idea to run off to New Mexico, remember? But the ranch is very important to you. Besides, I've done a lot recently to take you away from it. We'll go back anytime you say."

With those words tossed back over her shoulder, she sat down at the dressing table and began to struggle through the tangles in her hair.

Still Clay was not convinced. He called Shorty after breakfast and told him they were on their way home. Then they began making their way back across Texas, Kristen sleeping soundly on his shoulder. True, she had not been upset about not remaining longer in Santa Fe, and she had said she was looking forward to seeing the ranch. Still
. . .

He looked down at the sleeping face so close to his and a frown creased his forehead. He wanted so desperately to make her happy; what if inadvertently he had done the one thing that would destroy her happiness completely?

As if sensing his distress, Kristen's eyes opened. "What's wrong, Clay?" she asked. "Why are you frowning? Is something wrong?" She started to straighten up, but he smiled reassuringly, pressing her head back onto his shoulder.

"Nothing's wrong, sweetheart," he told her. "Just doing some heavy thinking." But when her eyes closed again, his frown returned.

They stopped to spend the night along the way, for Clay did not want to arrive at the ranch in the middle of the night. He wanted everything to go as well as possible and everything always seemed worse in the night.

The next day, as they neared the ranch, Clay found

himself growing more and more apprehensive. Recalling his and Shorty's housekeeping, or rather their lack of it, Clay envisioned Kristen's reaction to what had formerly been a bachelor household.

Perhaps he should have waited, come home later and given Shorty more time. But it was too late now. The gate was in sight and Kristen had seen it and was hopping about on the seat with excitement.

She turned to him, her eyes shining. "We're home, Clay!"

If his smile was weak, she was too excited to notice.

The road after they had turned off the highway was narrow and lined on either side with sumac bushes now turning bright autumn red, breathtakingly beautiful against the cedars. The tall oaks were changing to their russet browns and deep reds, but Clay saw little of their actual color.

When he pulled up before the old two-story rock house, he heard her swift intake of breath. With great reluctance he turned to see exactly what that meant and relief poured over him when he found her eyes fairly sparkling their delight.

"Oh, Clay," she breathed, "you didn't tell me about this."

"It needs a lot of fixing up," he warned her.

"Of course it does—that's part of the fun!" she said over her shoulder as she fairly leaped out of the car and bounded up the porch steps before he could stop her and prepare her for the worst. But he could have spared himself all the anxiety. On entering the house he found a note from Shorty saying that he was sure the newlyweds would prefer some time alone. He had gone to stay with the Moores but would be around the next day to help with the work. Lorene had left supper.

And she had done a lot more besides, Clay thought to himself as he looked at the house, clean and shining.

Again relief washed over him as he followed Kristen through the house, listening to her exclamations and plans.

But it was only after they had spent the entire day seeing the ranch that he finally began to relax. The sun was setting as they drove the pickup to the top of a hill and climbed up to stand looking out over the ranch. Their ranch, Kristen said, theirs and Shorty's, of course. There was a note of pride in her voice.

After a while they walked over to a grassy spot nestled within a cluster of evergreens where the scent of cedar surrounded them, strong yet pleasant. They settled there to watch the sunset and the coming of night.

"You're really happy, Kristen?" Clay sought to reassure himself.

She looked at him as if he had said something incredibly fantastic. "Clay, believe me, I couldn't possibly be happier."

"No regrets about Mrs. Faraday and your work there?"

"Absolutely no regrets."

She looked about her and felt the quiet sensations of the twilight. The stars were beginning to sparkle their way into the deepening sky.

Never had she experienced such peace and yet at the same time such excitement. She could feel the same excitement radiating from Clay as she leaned toward him, felt his arms encircling her, easing her down until she lay looking up at him as he lowered himself to where his face hovered just above hers. In the gathering darkness she could sense more than see the look in his eyes. Already she was becoming aware of his moods and reactions, and she savored each new revelation of himself, each new intimacy they shared. Steadily they were becoming more and more a part of each other.

She lay gazing up at him, remembering how she had been here once before. How she had seen him with the stars filling the sky above him. How she had felt her breath quicken in just this way as his lips moved slowly, deeply upon hers. How she had heard him whisper his love for her. And she had pushed his love away. Never, never again. Now her arms opened to wrap themselves around him, to pull him down until his full weight was on her, ready in the soft night to give herself again to him.

Now as his fingers worked through the buttons of her clothing there was no embarrassment. As each garment fell away, so it seemed to her did all sense of restraint or anxiety. As his hands touched and caressed, her body responded to his with eagerness and anticipation. She murmured her love for him between kisses that were causing the stars overhead to whirl crazily. They shared their love with the soft rustle of the night breeze overhead and the pungent scent of the blanket of cedar beneath them.

Sometime later, as she lay quietly, his arms wrapped closely around her against the cool of the evening, she heard him sigh with contentment.

"You'll never doubt my happiness again, will you?" she asked him. "You will never doubt that I'm exactly where I want to be?"

His arms tightened about her. She could hear the lilt of laughter in his voice and knew that all his former tensions had drained away.

"Not as long as you keep convincing me in such a thorough and most enjoyable manner."

**LOOK FOR NEXT MONTH'S
CANDLELIGHT ECSTASY ROMANCES:**

THE TAMING

Aleen Malcolm

Cameron—daring, impetuous girl/woman who has never known a life beyond the windswept wilds of the Scottish countryside.

Alex Sinclair—high-born and quick-tempered, finds more than passion in the heart of his headstrong ward Cameron.

Torn between her passion for freedom and her long-denied love for Alex, Cameron is thrust into the dazzling social whirl of 18th century Edinburgh and comes to know the fulfillment of deep and dauntless love.

A Dell Book $3.25

Love—the way you want it!

Candlelight Romances

Dell Bestsellers